RED MITTENS

a novel by

JEANINE LOVE ROONEY

Red Mittens

Authored by Jeanine Love Rooney
Edited by Tracy C. Ertl

Published by TitleTown Publishing
Green Bay, WI
www.titletownpublishing.com

Interior design by Euan Monaghan
Cover design by Travis J. Vanden Heuvel
Cover photo © TitleTown Publishing. ALL RIGHTS RESERVED

Publisher's note:
This story, including names, characters, places, and incidents, is a work of imaginative fiction, but based on true events. Some names and identifying details have been changed for privacy reasons. The author alone bears responsibility for any remaining errors in the text, which are wholly unintentional.

ISBN (hardcover): 978-1-949042-02-3
ISBN (paperback): 978-1-949042-03-0
This title is also available in electronic and audiobook formats.

PUBLISHER'S CATALOGING-IN-PUBLICATION DATA
Love Rooney, Jeanine
Red Mittens / Jeanine Love Rooney
1st edition. Green Bay, WI: TitleTown Publishing, c2018.

Proudly Printed in the United States of America
10 9 8 7 6 5 4 3 2 1

PROLOGUE

1990—Somewhere 'near' Providence, Rhode Island

GINA PERCHED ABOUT MIDWAY up the bleachers among the crowd of celebrants and well-wishers, anxiously scanning the field beyond and below … and hoping. Attendees filtered into the Crossroads complex, crossing the glittering surface of the oval track, picking their way across the vivid green sward of soft grass at its center.

Some peeled off and made their way to the bleachers. The others—Gina sighed—the *lucky* others, joined the small host seated on the grass at this end of the oval, facing a brilliantly white concert shell that looked just like the Hollywood Bowl, but much grander and more opulent.

At the bottom of the broad, equally white steps that fanned out from the concert shell, sat a low dais that appeared to be made of clear glass … or a chunk of perfect crystal.

It looked like any commencement ceremony, except the participants were clad in every conceivable style of clothing and ranged in age from toddlers to grandparents, though most appeared to be in their teens, twenties or thirties.

Well, another noticeable difference was that the turf was greener than any natural grass and the track looked as if it were made of

3

ground garnets and hematite. The "sunlight" fell from everywhere at once, bathing everything in incandescence, casting no shadows.

Gina smoothed the fabric of her cotton dress over her knees, as a sweet summery breeze laden with the scent of jasmine and orange blossoms caught and lifted the full skirt. Splashy red flowers on a field of white covered her whimsical sleeveless dress. In contrast, the woman seated next to her wore a teal silk suit with a pencil thin skirt and a pillbox hat. Looked like she'd raided Jackie Kennedy-Onassis's closet or been caught in a Goodwill time-warp. Who the heck wore pillbox hats anymore? It was nineteen-freaking-ninety.

I bet her breeze smells like Chanel No, 5, Gina thought. She almost asked the woman how long she'd been here, but decided that would be rude. Once upon a time she wouldn't have cared about behaving badly. In fact, she'd have reveled in it. She'd changed in the almost twenty years she'd spent here.

Gina frowned at the stragglers below on the track.

No Margo.

Again.

She supposed she shouldn't be surprised. This was—what—the fourth or fifth time they'd applied for passes and Margo hadn't shown. They'd argued about it repeatedly and, every time, Margo offered excuses, reasons that were ambiguous and grey.

A cluster of four girls in the group down on the field looked up at her, waving from the front row. The cheerleaders.

Gina smiled brightly and waved back, then blew kisses. She snuffed out the niggle of sadness at the sight of their radiant faces. She felt happy for them, she told herself fiercely. They were crossing over, passing on.

Someday I will too.

But not without Margo. She could go nowhere without

Margo. They were bound together by friendship and circumstances of life and death.

The hubbub of voices quieted as four figures in cream-colored robes and black rope belts appeared at the top of the steps within the concert shell, facing the congregation in the field. As the quartet descended the steps, Deb, the head cheerleader, and her companions sat down and faced front.

One of the robed, cowled officials beckoned the girls to ascend the stairs.

Gina leaned forward in her seat. This part always freaked her out, but she watched anyway, because someday that would be her up there, receiving a final benediction before leaving this place, never to return. Today, if Margo had bothered to come, they would at least have gotten visitor's passes to the destination where the four cheerleaders were headed.

Gina tried to imagine it: remembering her past but not being trapped by it, not feeling guilt over it, not wanting to take it all back ... or relive it. She tried to imagine being with Carlos, who had God only knew how long, to live. She dreamed of embracing him in a completely different way than she had interacted with him before.

She felt a swift stab of resentment at Margo for holding them here. For being unwilling to move on. She reined it in—hard. Resentment and recrimination would only get in the way. That had been her lesson to learn: seeking to place blame was a chimera. Circumstance was a collaborative invention.

Gina squinted in the shimmer of ambient light, remembering the fight she'd had with Margo the day before.

"I applied again," Gina informed her. "You told me it was all right, if you recall."

Margo merely shrugged. "We'll see. I'm still—you know—not sure I'm finished here."

"You mean you're not done with holding on to whatever it is you're grasping so desperately," Gina challenged, but Margo only changed the subject.

"I plan to set off the Francis Hall alarm at three AM on the night of the anniversary," she reported. "Freak out the residents. Come watch."

It was hard for Gina to believe her brainy roommate—Margo, the straight and upright—now got her kicks from haunting the unsuspecting students of Christopher Hayes Preparatory School.

Their guide, Thomas, had explained to them that the Halfway region facilitated transformation and sorting things out. Margo had changed all right, but not in a way Gina understood or could have expected. As much as it pained her to admit it, she had always depended on Margo's moral compass to keep her from going off the deep end. Margo was her anchor, but her anchor had lost its hold.

She didn't pretend to know why Margo struggled so much sorting things out. As tempting as it was to blame her attachment to earth—she knew there was more to it than that. Thomas had explained on their first day here that remorse was the hardest emotion for people to reconcile. Gina had plenty to be regretful about, but Margo?

Gina shook her head, her eyes going to the field below where the four cheerleaders stood before the members of the Soul Cleansing Board preparing to receive their Keys to the Kingdom. That's not what the Board called them, of course, but Gina always thought of them that way.

Who'd have thunk it? she reflected. *Who'd have picked Margo to transform from geeky straight girl to troubadour ghost, freaking out high school girls, whispering sweet nothings in her wannabe-boy-friend's ear, and spooking science track nerds by snuffing out Bunsen burners.*

Three of the robed figures were moving now, making Gina sit up in her bleacher seat, squinting to see. A chorus of angelic voices rose in song, the chord moving, shifting, rising and making Gina's entire being thrum like the strings of a violin.

And I thought sex was something.

The chord lifted her up, buoyed her, and filled her spirit. She wanted to close her eyes in bliss, but she couldn't miss this next part.

The four Board members—each standing before one of Gina's ex-dorm mates—reached into their robes and brought forth a point of gleaming light that seemed to be no color and all colors at once. The breathtaking light (at least it would have been, if anyone had breath to take) shimmered gloriously, and filled Gina with desire so strong she wanted to cry out with longing for that brilliant spark.

Around her, other members of the audience sang or sighed or laughed or wept, and Gina understood—as she did every time she witnessed the ceremony—that they all shared the same blaze of emotion.

The Board members took their little orbs of glory and pressed them into the hearts of the girls standing before them. From the heart of each girl, the light spread, suffusing every atom, making over every molecule, every cell of their already incorporeal bodies, into a mirror image of its own shining nature. The angelic choir, which was present as a halo of bril-liance above the field, modulated the chord. Gina wanted to swoon with joy.

From a watcher's perspective, the four girls began to climb the stairs even as the transformation progressed. The light devoured them until only a vaguely human-shaped aura of radiance remained, until even that became a cloud of shimmering motes, until even that disappeared.

The choir fell silent. The silence throbbed with equal parts loss and contentment. Gina felt tears racing down cheeks that might have hurt from smiling if they had been composed of flesh and blood and muscle, and not memory. Someday, she promised herself, someday that would be her and Margo going to the Light. But first, she knew, she had to understand why Margo kept them here in Halfway—stranded between Heaven and Earth.

PART I

"SHE CAME FROM PROVIDENCE,
THE ONE IN RHODE ISLAND..."

— THE EAGLES

1

Fall 1976

PRACTICE ENDED WITH THE coach calling for twenty laps around the gym. Eddie finish near the front of the pack and led the way to the locker room. The sweaty boys stripped out of their tank tops, sneakers and shorts, tossing them at the bottom of their lockers. They headed for the showers, cranking the nozzles up to their full heat and pressure. Soon the small room filled with steam.

"Anybody up for twenty-five cent fountain drinks at Dempsey's tonight?" yelled Doug, the brawny point guard.

"Not me," Eddie answered. "I've gotta meet my new tutor at the library in fifteen minutes. Maybe I'll catch up with you later."

"Another victim, I mean tutor," Doug laughed. "How soon before she writes your papers in exchange for a piece of you?"

"She's only human." Eddie responded. "Let's hope she doesn't know my reputation."

News traveled fast through the school—Eddie was NBA

material. The Hayes center knew pro scouts would be scoping him out. Maintaining his GPA at the scholarship minimum was the only obstacle he had faced between last year and now, two weeks into his junior season.

Eddie pulled his book bag from his locker and took out the file marked *Tutor: Margo Tracey*. Pre-med track.

Same drill, he thought. The tutors procured by the disgruntled prep school counselors wanted nothing more than to see a cocky jock trip up. But they were Eddie's ticket to a college scholarship. He had charmed his way into a string of tutors' hearts with his flirtations. In return, the bright women provided him all sorts of tests in advance, falsified study reports—jeopardizing their own academic status for the chance to win his approval and be accepted in his world. He would flatter this one, too, and invite her to Dempsey's Diner for a night of adoration. Then, after a few weeks of his sappy sweet talk, she, like all the others before her, would succumb.

Eddie walked through the night-quiet campus. The brisk breeze held promise in the air as it signaled the upcoming cold New England winter, his favorite season. He picked up his pace as he passed cluttered areas of congregating students. Ignoring the aroma of pizza wafting on the breeze, Eddie resolutely turned right, and climbed the library steps.

Once inside, he looked around for a redhead in a forest green t-shirt to match his counselor's description of Margo. He spotted her almost immediately, sitting at an otherwise empty table near the front of the large outer study hall. He sized her up as he moved closer. She'd have been a knockout if she knew how to dress herself. Too many freckles, but he thought her vivid hair and freckles blended into the rose of her cheeks in a way that made her pretty.

Red Mittens

* * *

Margo checked the clock over the librarian's desk and noticed a tall, ruddy guy with broad shoulders and curly blonde hair walking toward her. Eddie's reputation preceded him. Margo's counselor had warned her about his escapades. Girls, especially his prior tutors, loved him. And she could see why. He was good-looking, yes, but his obvious self-confidence really added to his allure. Eddie appeared easy in his body, comfortable in his own skin. She caught herself gazing at his muscular arms and looked down quickly at the history class syllabus as her face reddened. When he spoke, his smooth, deep voice startled her.

"I hear a man can learn a little something about history in these parts," Eddie chuckled, and slid into the seat directly across from her. His legs sprawled below the table from one end to the other.

"Where are your books?" she asked.

She caught his eye roll as she reached into her knapsack and pulled out her history text.

"I don't need books," he explained. "I have a photographic memory. I'm not as dumb as you may think. How about ditching this place and going to Dempsey's for a Coke?"

She slowly and deliberately took out a pencil. "Who said anything about you being dumb? I have to pass on your offer, though. I'm not into drinking liquid sugar in a crowded diner on a school night ... I bet you think my reasoning sounds kind of strange."

"I don't gamble, and strange is underrated." His eyes locked with hers. "I'm not sounding dumb now, am I?"

Man, he's smooth. She gazed back at him, not wanting to be the first one to blink.

He sighed and rolled his eyes again. "Strange or not strange. Take me up on Dempsey's. Let's study there."

"Studying amid the din of pinball machines and blaring rock'n'roll. That's creative."

"Yeah, I know. If you saw my grades from last year, you'd think I took my finals buried under an pool table."

Good looking and *funny*. She bounced her pencil on the text book. "Back to the Civil War. You're stuck with me for the next ninety minutes. I don't fudge tutor time sheets and I don't lay down cover for anybody. So why don't you borrow my book and we can start with Lincoln's speech? Chapter Four, page five," she instructed, cocking her eyebrow. "I have plenty of paper. I suggest you start taking notes."

Eddie laughed softly and relented. He found her quiet determination oddly endearing.

They had covered all the upcoming quiz topics, when they were interrupted by a tall blonde who stopped at the table. "Hey, Eddie, I'm on my way to Dempsey's, wanna come?"

"Sure. I think we were just wrapping up." Eddie responded, looking at Margo. "Right?"

"Yes, we were just finishing," Margo agreed. "Have a blast." What was the use of trying to mold him so quickly into a disciplined student? *He'll come around.*

Eddie stood up and sauntered out with the blonde, leaving Margo with *The History of Western Civilization*, her spiral bound notebooks, and a feeling of unexplained isolation.

* * *

As Gina walked down the dormitory steps and around the building's corner into the quad, she spied her roommate, Amy, with her head down, approaching the dorm from the other end. Amy seemed to be in a hurry. She sported a white tube top and worn out overalls with holes in the knees. Long blue feather earrings peeked out from the long, fine brown hair tucked behind her ears. Gina marveled at how Amy managed to turn a second rate wardrobe into high fashion.

Out of breath when she reached Gina, Amy exclaimed, "I am so excited! It's Dempsey's tonight! I wish they'd let us off the reservation more often."

"Me too. We better get a move on." Gina tugged her sweater closer to her body. They walked across the quad, through the parking lot, out the fancy wrought iron gate, and down Yarmouth Street where Dempsey's, the cornerstone student diner, served as a landmark for years, nestled between a 7-Eleven and Gary's Pizzeria.

The two roommates waited at the back of a line twenty students deep outside on Dempsey's front deck. Gina checked her reflection in the diner's front window — a blur with dark hair and huge dark eyes, wearing a bright blue mini dress. She noticed a tall guy in the front of the line eyeing her legs. The one behind him followed suit.

Gina smiled … then out of the corner of her eye, she noticed her boyfriend, Carlos, striding toward her. Dressed in a tweed sports coat and loafers, he looked ready for a seminar, not a noisy teen hangout. But he was gorgeous in a professorial sort of way, with his wavy black hair and wire rimmed glasses.

"What are you doing here?" Gina asked as she kissed him on the cheek.

"I stopped by your dorm to take you to a poetry reading hosted by one of my buddies and somebody mentioned you came here with your roommate. So what do you say, can I pull you away from meaningless gab for a night of spiritual enlightenment?"

"I kinda had my heart set on gab and a soda. Do you want to join us?" Gina offered, trying to sound more enthusiastic than she felt. It wasn't that she didn't want his company, she just didn't know how well Carlos would fit in with the younger crowd. He was a college man—twenty years to Gina's sixteen—and acted as if he were professor emeritus.

"I guess I could come in for a while." He took Gina's hand in his and squeezed it. She felt a touch of excitement, then a pang of guilt for her earlier lack of enthusiasm. After all, Carlos had been responsible for bringing her to her sexual awaking this past summer.

Carlos had been gentle, and very patient—taking more liberties each night, teaching Gina to respond to his romantic advances, easing her past any virgin awkwardness.

"You must let go," he would insist. "You mustn't be afraid of passion."

And she wasn't afraid. Each night Carlos urged her on, until at last, Gina found herself responding with matched zeal. Afterwards she would beg, "Let's go for a moonlight stroll, let's count the stars, let's go to your studio and run wild." But Carlos rarely wanted to venture out.

They'd had the talk about giving each other more space, seeing if their relationship could stand the test of time and freedom. Once, over the summer, Gina had slipped out for a few nights with a soft spoken North Dakota boy. He wanted her, which fueled her desire for him. They'd kissed, and she found herself relinquishing her body to a boy she hardly knew. But soon she'd torn away from him and fled back to Carlos, who had noticed the drift but made light of it. He acted like the owner of a curious puppy, who looked the other way when his pet strayed into a neighbor's yard.

Gina enjoyed a dual existence. Spending time with Carlos, she played the role of the sophisticated would-be artiste student in awe of the worldly guru who had seduced her when he'd sat in on her summer art class. They'd painted and sculpted together; he'd given her private sketch lessons, taken care of her. At Christopher Hayes Prep, two weeks into her sophomore year, she regarded Carlos as a far away treasure floating further and further out to sea. Her personal attachment waned once she discovered the theatre studs who strolled across campus with beatnik cool, or the baseball players whose biceps bulged out of their t-shirts when they reached for mashed potatoes in the school cafeteria line.

"Hey, we're next in line," Amy shook her out of her trance.

"Look at the size of this guy," Carlos remarked as Eddie Sullivan ducked his head to keep from beaning himself on the front door frame.

"He's gorgeous," Amy sighed. "I've seen him around campus in those tight basketball shorts. I wonder if he has a girlfriend."

"Margo told me this morning she was meeting him at the library tonight. She's tutoring him," Gina said.

"Lucky her," Amy replied. "I'd like to teach him a thing or two."

"Okay, girls. We're up" Carlos nudged.

Inside, a long counter and a clutter of small tables and booths took center stage. Tucked away in the back was a pool table, a row of arcade games and pinball machines, and a juke box, which, right now, played Van Morrison. Most of the students crammed together at the counter chugging milkshakes and sodas. Dempsey's had officially kicked off a new year at CHP.

Carlos got a soda, whispered, "Don't go far, Pet. I'll be watching you," then made his way to the pool table.

Gina and Amy wound their way to the counter and ordered a pitcher of root beer.

"Whaddaya think?" Gina asked Amy. "What a place! What a vibe! All these students cutting loose."

"I don't know how much cutting loose you'll be doing with your boyfriend here."

"Good point."

Amy gave her a friendly pat on the back. "Let's go over to the corner of the counter. This could be interesting."

"Let me guess," Gina said, "the group Eddie Sullivan is standing with?"

"You bet."

"Have it your way." Gina followed her roommate past a group of guys in rugby shirts and gym shorts downing Cokes and trying to out-shout one another with songs about team spirit, girls, and rugby. The girls leaned up against the counter.

* * *

Eddie Sullivan reclined in the rear of the diner alternating between sips of coffee and cold water. He wracked his brain trying to think of the name of the song playing on the jukebox.

"Slip me a dollar for a few ginger ales." Eddie's roommate Doug implored, holding his hand out.

"Hell, you got the most expensive sneakers on the team, but you don't have enough money to pay for your own goddamn ginger ale?" Eddie asked incredulously.

"It's on me." The guy behind the counter leaned across with two bottles.

"Thanks, man," Doug replied appreciatively.

"Ditto," Eddie chimed in.

The guy nodded at Eddie. "You just keep winning those tip-offs and banging the backboards and you can have all the soda pop you want. Bring the championship trophy back to CHP this year."

Eddie felt a light tap on his shoulders and turned.

"Hi. I'm Amy. A little birdie told me my roommate Margo is your tutor. This is my other roommate, Gina."

Eddie looked at Amy and found it hard to imagine she roomed with his uptight tutor. "Yeah, Margo is helping me with a little history. Matter of fact, I should be home studying."

"Don't worry. Your secret's safe with me," Amy confided with a wink.

* * *

One of the guys standing to Eddie's right whispered in Gina's ear. "I'm Mike, Captain of the rugby team. Welcome to the sporting corner of the establishment."

"I'm Gina," she replied. Out of the corner of her eye, she watched Carlos line up a shot at the pool table.

"I'm hitting the jukebox," Amy whispered in her other ear. "I'll pick a slow song and maybe Eddie will ask me to dance."

Gina poured herself another cup of root beer from the pitcher and made room for Mike to inch closer.

"I haven't seen you around," he said.

Gina gave a forced laugh. "I'm a sophomore. I transferred in at the beginning of the year."

"Cool," Mike said. "How about a sundae? It's on me."

"Sounds great," Gina smiled.

After several minutes of ice cream, idle chatter and flirting, Gina began to unwind. Then she felt a firm tug on her arm.

"I guess I can't leave you unattended even long enough to play a round of pool," Carlos barked. "Let's get out of here."

Gina pulled her arm away. "I'm not ready to go."

"I see ... now I have to compete with a bunch of rock heads for your attention?"

Mike leaned in. "Who you calling a rock head, old man? I didn't know you had a chaperone," he added in a loud aside to Gina.

"Excuse us. I think we need to get some fresh air," Gina side-stepped, gently guiding Carlos through the restaurant.

"Listen," Gina explained, once they were outside and out of earshot of the students hanging around on the outdoor deck and patio, "I want to stay a while longer with Amy. I'll call you from the dorm when I get home."

Carlos's hazel eyes flashed angrily behind his glasses. "I see where this is going," he wheeled around abrubtly. "Have a nice evening." He strode off without kissing her goodbye.

She almost followed after him, but then she heard a favorite song start up on the jukebox and a girl's peal of laughter called her back into the diner.

Dempsey's closed at 10:00 PM as usual, but Gina suspected that the night with Mike wasn't going to end here.

"We're having a late-night stealth keg party at our house. Wanna come?" Mike invited.

Before Gina could answer, Amy reappeared, inquiring, "Are you ready to go? Eddie and a bunch of the guys are heading next door for pizza so we can be back at Francis Hall by eleven."

"I'll catch you back at Francis Hall," Gina responded, giving Mike a meaningful glance.

Amy looked from Gina to Mike and back. "All right," Amy agreed. "Don't do anything I wouldn't do."

Mike took Gina's hand and maneuvered through the crowded diner until they emerged into the cool night air.

Soon the other rugby players and the girls they had picked up joined them. Together, everyone noisily paraded down Yarmouth Street. Gina and Mike let the others pass and trailed behind, holding hands and intentionally brushing against each other.

Mike and several of his teammates shared a rental on Yarmouth Street, just outside the lower campus gate of the boarding school. They were seniors and had no live-in chaperone—ideal for the occasional kegger. Gina and Mike followed the others up the broad front steps and into the spacious living room. Mike reached into his pocket and pulled out a twenty, stuffing it into the goldfish bowl where his teammate was collecting party donations. Then, he gestured to Gina to sit on a worn love-seat. She sank into the cushions and looked around. Except for the stereo, the eclectic decor —two other sofas and a couple of beanbag chairs —had seen better days.

The next few hours passed in a haze of alcohol, cigarette smoke, and weed. Mike and Gina slow-danced while he whispered into her ear, "Let's go to my room."

They wended their way through the living room and down the hall to the first door on the left. A double mattress nestled in the corner of the bedroom, and bookcases made of cinderblocks and planks lined the walls. Dirty clothes lay scattered around the floor. A small lamp, with rays so feeble they illuminated barely more than a nightlight, gave the room a soft glow.

Mike kissed Gina. Her hand rested on his biceps, which bulged against the fabric of his shirt and pulled tight against his muscular chest. He backed her up against the wall and leaned into her. The heat in her body rose and she let herself forget where she should have been at the moment—where she really wanted to be, if she was honest with herself—and let her body take over. Mike guided her onto the bed while Grateful Dead music pulsed through the house.

Moments later, they heard a loud banging on the bedroom window.

Mike rolled over. "Who the hell is that?"

Gina sat up. *I know damn well who it is.*

Backlit by the lights of the campus parking lot, she saw a silhouette that could only be one person. She buttoned up her dress, grabbed her purse, and looked at Mike sheepishly.

"Who's the guy outside?" he demanded. "Is that the older dude that was hanging around you at Dempsey's? What's his deal?

"Sorry, but I better go."

She slipped out of the bedroom, through the living room and out the front door, scanning for him as she stepped onto the sidewalk. "I know you're out here, Carlos. I can't believe you're spying on me."

Out of the corner of her eye, she saw him appear from the side yard and ran to him, fists clenched, with every intention of pummeling his handsome face. Instead, she fell into his arms and sobbed.

He didn't hold her; he pushed her away. "You're right," he admitted. "I can't believe I've reduced myself to standing outside of some jock's window watching him get ready to screw my girlfriend. You know, I actually thought you were serious about just spending the night out with your friends. You must think I'm a complete moron. What are we doing here, Gina? Are you my girlfriend or aren't you? If you want your freedom—just say the word."

She punched him in the chest, panicked at the thought that he would leave her. "No, don't go. I need you." Then she closed her eyes and whispered to herself, *I also need my freedom. Even just a taste would do.*

* * *

The broad fourth floor corridor of Francis Hall dormitory served as Margo's sanctuary. Tonight, it was crowded with her dorm neighbors. Deb, the captain of the cheerleading squad, doled out step charts for the squad's latest choreography routine, the three Swedish runners talked about strategy for an upcoming meet, and Anya, the Resident Advisor, lounged on the couch eating potato chips straight out of the bag. Amy and Gina were off at Dempsey's.

Margo tossed a black and white pom-pom off the arm of her chair and dove into her biology book, inhaling the heady perfume of molecular modeling. Her mind kept coming back to her afternoon study session with Eddie. She feared she had come off like an uppity know-it-all sophomore, when in reality she had achieved so much because of her focus and determination. She had been at the top of her class since middle school and remembered her commencement speech like it was yesterday. In it, she'd pledged to be the first female surgeon in Rhode Island and urged her classmates to avoid the trappings of the high school party life so that they could return home to their humble roots in Middletown, Rhode Island, with banners screaming their successes.

Margo, an only child whose parents sacrificed to send her to a private preparatory high school, worked harder than anyone. The partial academic scholarship helped, but her middle school counselor warned her that the bulk of college scholarship funds went to athletes. Shooting a basket had more monetary value than medical school potential. Eddie had a full ride. And where was he now? Probably not at the library.

* * *

Eddie yanked a napkin from the counter at Gary's Pizzeria and wiped the grease from his face, checking the clock over the front door. His team curfew of 11:00 PM quickly approached. Stopping at the phone booth outside, he dialed his dorm neighbor and teammate, Chuck Turner.

"Hey, Turner. It's Sullivan. When Coach calls you, let him know I'm running fifteen minutes late. I'll check in when I get back."

"Sure. Whaddaya got that's making you put in overtime? That stacked trombone player who's always shadowing you around the student union? She's got it bad for you. Oh, hey, before I forget, Coach actually stopped by the dorm looking for you while you were with your tutor." He said the last two words with a sly smirk in his voice.

Eddied ignored it. "Oh shit. What did I do wrong now?"

"Just the opposite. Says he got wind a Celtics scout might be at a game this season to see you, so don't screw up. I know you're Irish—what's your lucky charm?"

Good question, Eddie thought as he hung up. But the question wasn't *what* his lucky charm was, but who. He headed north, toward campus.

* * *

Finishing her homework, Margo looked up to watch the girls playing Charades in between catching pieces of popcorn in their mouths. Gina and Amy had just returned home and sat cross-legged on either side of her.

"How was Dempsey's?" Margo asked.

"I met Eddie. What a great guy ... and Gina, well, she had quite the adventure ... and quite her pick of men." She leered at Gina.

Gina stood up to act out her Charade. "Adventure? That's an understatement. I will save the gory details for later tonight when we're under the covers and can't sleep."

"I can hardly wait," Margo laughed.

Before Gina could begin acting out her Charade, Anya, the RA, shoved a pile of message pad notes into her hands. "Considering we've only been here a few weeks, Gina, you sure are making an impression on the guys. You got five calls downstairs at the main desk while you were out."

"I guess I need to hire a secretary to sit in our room and answer the phone," Gina laughed. She dropped the notes into Margo's lap and mimicked Marilyn Monroe well enough that another player guessed it right away. "You're up next, Amy."

"Anya can take my turn," Amy remarked. "I want to talk to Margo." She turned and whispered, "I met Eddie Sullivan tonight. I know you tutor him. What's he like?"

"Persuasive ... not on me, but, you know... on others ... like his teachers and prior tutors, I've heard."

"I can see why." Amy grabbed a potato chip from Anya's untended bag. "Maybe you should cut him some slack. He's got the weight of the season on him. High expectations from the coach, from his many fans—heck, from the whole school."

"I never thought of it that way," Margo murmured quietly.

"I find him *fascinating*," Amy bubbled, fluttering her lashes. "But if you like him, I can stay away." She lifted a hand to her forehead and sighed dramatically.

"Our relationship is strictly business. Don't let me stand in your way."

Margo heard their dorm room phone ring. Amy jumped up, opened the door, and reached around to snag the receiver. Then she stretched the cord out to the hall.

"Sure thing," Amy noted, mugging at Margo, wide-eyed. "I'll let her know." She hung up the phone and looked at Margo. "Eddie Sullivan is downstairs to see you."

Margo scurried off like a scalded cat.

Eddie stood loitering near the front desk.

"Everything okay?" she asked. "Do you need something for history class tomorrow?"

Dressed in the same outfit as earlier, jeans and a t-shirt, he now seemed a little disheveled. Hurried.

"No, I'm good with history, all set until our next session. I stopped by to ask you to go for a walk."

What an unexpected turn of events.

As if he sensed her hesitation, he added, "Don't worry. We'll keep it academic and talk about John Calhoun's Southern Address to your heart's content."

"So you *have* been doing some reading on your own. Good for you. Okay, I'm game."

"Cool. The campus coffee shop is still open—it makes a mean cup of black."

As they walked across the quad, leaves floated down from the plentiful maples and wild apple trees, looking like huge, golden snowflakes in the warm yellow of the campus lamps.

"I think you're my good luck charm," Eddie suddenly blurted out.

Margo stopped dead in her tracks and stared at him as he gazed off toward the gymnasium. "What? What do you mean?"

"When my counselor told me you were my tutor, in the same breath he surprised me with the news that the athletic department had increased my scholarship to cover extra items like additional notebooks and travel. Then, this afternoon, while we were studying at the library, an NBA scout called my coach to get our schedule so he could see me this coming season."

"Coincidence," Margo explained as she kicked the leaves. "Or miracle. Either way, I'm sure it's not me."

"Don't know, but I feel like I'm on a lucky streak and you may have something to do with it. I want you to hold onto this." He pulled something out of the front pocket of his jeans and held it out to her, balanced on the palm of his hand. A man's ring with an oversized ruby inset sparkled in the lamp light as he offered it up. "It's my sophomore year championship ring."

When she didn't take it, he gently grabbed her hand and pressed the ring into it. Her hand felt clumsy with the awkward shape stuck to her palm. Her fingers instinctively wrapped around it.

He's so unscientific, she thought. *All this nonsense about luck.* She opened her mouth to explain the theory of athletics and genetics, versus the power of a rabbit's foot, but surprised herself by promising, "I'll guard it with my life."

She shoved him playfully and, as he tripped and tumbled into the leaves, he grabbed her arm to pull her down with him. She struggled to get up, but he pulled her closer.

"I want to kiss you," he told her.

She laughed. "I bet you say that to all the tutors."

"But this time I think I feel something more."

"I don't believe you."

"Give it time."

"Fine." She tugged away from him and rolled to her feet, swatting leaves out of her hair. "We've got all the time in the world."

2

IT HAD BEEN THREE months since Margo had begun tutoring Eddie, and first semester finals were rapidly approaching.

Eddie and I have so much to cover tonight, she thought. *I don't want to be late.*

But the Francis Hall fourth floor bathroom at 7:00 PM was a mob scene. The cold tile on her bare feet sent shivers up and down Margo's spine. The bathroom had a permanent chill about it. The wait for the shower normally wouldn't have bothered her, but tonight, ten girls paraded in and out of the bathroom to shower and dry their hair at the shared vanity.

Margo spied Gina stepping naked into the stall and rushed over to her. "Can I cut the line?" Margo pleaded. "I'm running late for my study session."

From her place in line, Amy called out, "You better let her cut, Gina. You don't want to keep the great Hayes Prep hoops hope waiting and make those blue eyes red."

Gina stepped back out of the stall and wrapped herself in a white terry cloth robe. "Ok. Take my spot. Don't tell me, let me guess … you're in a mad rush to cut up frogs in your beloved physics lab with Eddie."

"You don't dissect frogs in physics, Gina, and I'm tutoring Eddie in history," Margo patiently corrected, then interpreted the look on her friend's face. "Oh, ha-ha. Very funny."

Margo scooted past Gina. She showered quickly, barely registering that the water was lukewarm. She finished up and toweled off quickly, rushing back into the room to find Amy holding up the clothes Margo had set out on the vanity.

"Ooo-la-la," Amy teased. "Somebody's favorite beaded macramé sweater and Levis. The tutor has more than tutoring on her mind, and we have the proof." She frowned. "Margo, this sweater is still wet. You go out in this, you'll freeze your tits off."

"No problem," Margo responded, taking the sweater and jeans from her. "I'll just use the hairdryer. Does the trick every time."

Margo plugged in one of the hairdryers lying on the vanity, draped the sweater over a stand mirror, then used a jar of Noxzema to prop the dryer up so the jet of warm air aimed directly at the damp garment. Then she wriggled into her jeans.

Gina looked on approvingly. "Now, that's resourceful. You're a real loon, Margo Tracey."

Margo laughed as she zipped up her jeans. "Don't worry, you only have to put up with me until graduation."

Anya poked her head into the bathroom just then. "Hey Gina, your gentleman friend is here. I let him up—against my better judgment. He's waiting in your room. Don't let him stay too long or we'll both be in trouble."

"Thanks. He's painting me today. A nude portrait, actually." Gina's eyes twinkled.

"Far out," Amy commented.

"Sounds like a blast," Margo agreed. "I gotta run." She

plaited her hair into two quick braids, pulled on her mostly dry sweater, and scurried out of the bathroom.

* * *

Gina wondered why she bothered getting dressed up for a nude painting. Still, she donned a mini dress and lots of red lipstick, tied her hair into a thick black bun, and gave herself the once-over in the bathroom mirror. Sophistication personified.

She walked in to find Carlos sitting on her dorm room bed. "Ta-da," she announced, posing in the doorway so he could appreciate the full effect of her tiny skirt and long legs. When he didn't respond, she crossed the room to lean over and give him a big, wet kiss. "You look so handsome. I can't wait to get to your studio!"

Carlos jerked his head away and glared at her so furiously that she took a step back. He clenched a fistful of phone messages. "Your RA dropped off your phone messages while you and your roommates were in the bathroom," he spit out tersely. "You've got three of them: Don invited you to go for a motorcycle ride tonight. Joe came across a copy of the American Studies pop quiz for tomorrow and asked if you want to meet him in the library to pick it up. I assume you do. Oh, and I saved the best for last—Sam confirmed he'll pick you up tomorrow night at six for the Pink Floyd concert."

Gina felt a migraine forming behind her eyes. She didn't know what to say. What came out of her mouth was, "I don't take those offers seriously." She stared down at her shoes.

"Try saying that again, and this time look me in the eye," Carlos demanded.

She couldn't.

"As I suspected." He stood and dropped the incriminating messages onto the bed. "No sweat, really. We'll do the painting another time. When you're more focused."

Gina took his hand, but he pulled it away.

"I *am* focused. I *am* ready." She ran her hands over her breasts and down the middle of her stomach before stopping and pulling his hand to her breast. "Take me to bed," she whispered, closing her eyes and feeling the heat in her body swirl.

"Yes," Carlos groaned. "I want you. But I want it all. Not just pieces, at your convenience." He pulled his hand away and walked out the door, slamming it behind him.

"Don't go!" she cried. She opened the door to chase after him but he had already disappeared.

* * *

Margo sat at a table in the library waiting for CHPs' "hoops hope" to appear. Eddie was already twenty minutes late. Margo knew he needed to memorize the material for the Gettysburg Address if he wanted to pull even a C on the U.S. history final scheduled for next Tuesday,.

Shaking her head in annoyance, she began organizing her own notes for her next lab assignment—snake dissection—and settled into her favorite subject.

If only every subject could be this fascinating.

When she looked up, she realized that nearly two hours had passed. Only a few students remained in the library, busily packing up their gear, leaving piles of books on the study tables. The head librarian stood behind the main desk, sorting books and tidying up.

Dumping her books and notes into her bag, Margo joined the

exodus of students quietly filing out the front door. She tucked her hands into the sleeves of her fringed-suede jacket. Her last stop before returning to Francis Hall was a trip to the student union to collect her mail. Walking across the flood-lit path, she noticed how the light played up the late autumn colors of the maples.

Margo scaled the steps to the building two at a time and flung open one of the glass doors. Except for the sound of music and laughter emanating from Angie's the on-campus lounge, all was quiet. She stood in front of the wall of mailboxes, pulled the key from her pocket and stuck it into the lockbox to retrieve her mail. After sorting through letters from her parents, and leafing through the latest monthly edition of *National Geographic*, she opened the results of her mid-term biology exam.

Reading the words, she heard them in the slightly lisping German accent of her beloved biology teacher, Mr. Azzi: "Margo, I am sending you a copy of your latest test on proteins to let you know why this is a B minus. I know how you have strived and succeeded in receiving the highest class score on every test and pop quiz. If there is something going on or you want to talk, I am here for you."

There it was. Her grades were slipping. Eddie's fault, no doubt. She would find him and tell him that all her attention helping him pass history jeopardized her chance to go down in the history books as the first female surgeon in Rhode Island. She stopped by the glass wall of the student lounge to open a letter from her father. Glancing into the crowded room, Margo caught sight of Eddie and her roommate, Amy, in what seemed to be an intimate conversation.

Catching Margo's glare, Eddie and Amy waved, signaling for her to come in. Margo shook her head and watched him whisper into Amy's ear, then leave her to come out into the hall.

"Let me guess," Margo looked him in the eye. "Angie's is having a sale on Cheetos."

"Yeah," Eddie laughed. "Buy one, get twenty free."

"You stood me up tonight. You were supposed to meet me at the library at eight o'clock, "Margo pouted, hands pressed firmly on her hips. "You play basketball all day and party all night."

He chuckled. "It seemed to be a winning formula until I met you."

"I'm not amused," Margo muttered in a low voice.

"I'm sorry about tonight," Eddie apologized sheepishly. "I thought we were meeting *tomorrow* night." He quickly changed the subject. "Wow, you look almost sexy tonight. Let's talk about the calendar mix-up over a Coke."

Funny how it suddenly dawned on her that he was lying. He probably had been lying about everything all along.

"I don't like soda pop all that much," Margo snapped. "Call me when you're ready to study."

"Don't be mad, Margo. I'm sorry, really. Listen, we can study now. Let's go back to the library. I just have to grab my books from my dorm room. Let's go."

"What about Amy?" Margo asked, her eyes flicking back inside to the lounge.

"What?" Eddie wondered, looking truly perplexed. "Oh, that's nothing. We were just talking. She won't even notice I'm gone."

Margo let Eddie tug her across campus and over to his dorm. The Resident Advisor behind the reception counter had his back turned while chatting with someone. Eddie grasped her arm and hustled her to the staircase before the guy caught sight of them. She felt a tingle of unease at breaking dorm rules. As she opened her mouth to say something, Eddie put a finger to his lips to beg her silence. She bit her tongue.

"Welcome to my castle," he greeted, opening the door and guiding her inside his tiny single-occupant dorm room. "Have a seat." He pointed to the day bed near the wall on the opposite side of the room.

She plopped on the bed while Eddie flipped on the dusty stereo and rummaged through a basket of dirty clothes, basketballs, and books, until he came up with a history text.

"I won't screw up again with our library dates," Eddie assured her. "I'm coming clean. I blew you off tonight and I'm sorry."

"I knew you weren't telling me the truth," Margo pouted. "And then, trying to butter me up by telling me I look *almost* sexy." She blushed.

"*That* was the truth. And forget the 'almost.' You're totally sexy. Now, before we go to the library, let me be the tutor for a while."

His eyes studied her, strong, hard, and piercing. Margo knew she was entering forbidden territory and tempting fate. He reached out and gripped her knees.

"Move over."

He sat beside her, then gently pushed her back until she was resting on her elbows. Taking the bottom of the open-weave sweater in the tips of his fingers, he began to slide it upwards. He bent down and kissed her bare navel. The contrast of his hot mouth against her cold skin sent a shock through her system. He pulled her closer and positioned himself over her torso.

She tried to release her clumsiness in anticipation of the sensations to come: the weight, the pressure, his hands ready to explore her body. His lips pressed against her neck and throat. She closed her eyes and prepared herself for ecstasy.

In the distance, she thought she could hear the sound of a man's voice, crying out. A faraway voice.

3

WHEN THE ALARM WENT off, Margo woke with her everyday sense of purpose, but as she stretched, she felt a sudden stab of anxiety.

What was today?

She tossed the covers aside and stood up sleepily. The cold hardwood floor jarred her awake. She picked up her calendar from her desk. Ah, yes … this morning she'd meet with Eddie, his counselor, and Eddie's father to get a progress report of Eddie's pre-finals grades. She had been forewarned that he'd been passing most of his quizzes and showing some improvement, but that he needed nothing short of a miracle to shift his GPA over the scholarship minimum.

Eddie had applied himself slightly more over the past several weeks. Margo had noticed a tender expression on his face when he spoke about the sacrifices certain Americans made throughout history. His grasp of the material had increased. She was sure of it. Eddie held academic promise.

"I'll set your dad straight," she whispered aloud.

She chose a conservative bib dress, slipped on brown suede moccasins and tied her hair back with a rubber band.

Why are my hands trembling?

Margo dodged past students and faculty milling outside the counselors' offices. As she got ready to knock on Counselor Turner's door, it flew open, and the diminutive woman stepped out, coffee cup in hand.

"I need a refill before Eddie and his father arrive. Go on in and have a seat."

Margo sat down in one of the wing back chairs, feeling a knot growing in her stomach. A thick file entitled "Eddie Sullivan" in bold, black letters caught her eye. She was tempted to have a look inside, when Professor Turner returned, sat down, and took a long sip of her coffee. She put the cup down next to the file, shook her head and sighed.

"I guess we're going to be adding a few more pages to the Eddie Sullivan paper trail."

"Professor Turner, I've been trying to—"

"Don't worry. You can be quite certain that I don't blame you for Eddie's precarious status at CHP. His history teacher stopped by the other day and told me she had to wake him from a semi-coma the other morning just to provide him a D on a pop quiz." Professor Turner pointed to the file. "Judging from the bulk and bulging papers, you can deduce that he has a long history of dodging his studies in favor of other—shall we say—less educational activities. Part of Eddie's routine is to seduce his tutors who then, in turn, complete his homework assignments. I can tell you're not the type to fall into his trap, which is why I paired you with him in the first place."

Margo flushed hot and struggled to think of something to

say. Then she heard a sharp knock on the door. A stocky man in overalls and construction boots walked in, followed by Eddie. Margo guessed Eddie's height came from his mother's side of the family.

"Thank you for joining us, Mr. Sullivan. We're looking forward to giving you a status update on Eddie."

Professor Turner gestured toward the couch against the wall. Eddie kept his gaze directed at the wooden floorboards of Professor Turner's office.

Mr. Sullivan didn't waste his time with any niceties. "The coach told me that Eddie's scholarship is in jeopardy if he pulls anything less than a C this semester. I'm assuming you called this meeting to tell me he's pretty far from a C."

"I'm sorry," Professor Turner acknowledged, "but I'm afraid it's not good news."

Sullivan had noticed Margo. "Who's this?"

"Margo is Eddie's tutor. I asked her to come to give her assessment of Eddie's progress."

"You've given him an army of tutors and they've all ended up in bed with him."

Margo's face felt as if it were on fire. She feared raising her eyes to look at Eddie.

Turner ignored the crude accusation. "Margo's not your average tutor, Mr. Sullivan. She's a first-class student. One of our rising stars."

"Well, Eddie," Mr. Sullivan criticized. "Seems like the school gave you Madame Curie on a platter and you're still screwing up. You got anything to say?"

"No, sir, "Eddie murmured.

Mr. Sullivan grabbed Eddie's ear and lifted him off the sofa. Then, he made a fist and swung it into Eddie's midsection with enough force to knock the air out of him. Eddie collapsed on the floor.

Professor Turner leapt to her feet. "Mr. Sullivan, such violence is not permitted on this campus!"

"Look, lady, you wanted Eddie to come here to play basketball. You knew his grades weren't all that good in middle school. You committed to help him. Now, he may get thrown off the team and lose his scholarship, because all the help you can provide isn't enough for my son. You may not like my methods, but they're effective."

"With a little cooperation, Margo could be very helpful."

Grabbing Eddie by the arm, Mr. Sullivan hauled him upright. "I'll make sure he cooperates." He turned his head to look into Margo's eyes. "Just make sure that he nails his History final instead of you." He tugged his son toward the door.

"Eddie, meet me in the student lounge tonight," Margo called after them. She fled Turner's office, hiding her shaking hands in her pockets all the way to her dorm.

Margo passed the security guard at the front desk of Francis Hall, climbed four flights of stairs, and welcomed the familiar sight of her roommates sitting in a circle of girls in the middle of the hall. Gina and Amy, still dressed in their flannel pajamas, were munching on bags of potato chips and downing half pint cartons of orange juice.

Anya called out as Margo walked toward them: "It's our future doctor back from another early morning of hard-core studying. How did it go today in the biology lab? Did you dissect any rats with heart murmurs?"

"No rodent operations this morning, just a meeting with Professor Turner. But in an hour I've got a prep session with our agar plates." Margo mustered a fake smile. Her hands and insides had stopped shaking, but only just.

"Sounds dreamy," enthused Gina between gulps of orange juice.

Margo sat down cross-legged next to her. "And I can't wait for tomorrow," she gushed, realizing she was babbling, but unable to stop herself. "Our lab group has plans to spend all morning prepping for our next project—pig dissection. Pigs are a great human analogue."

"Just what we want to hear about while we're eating breakfast," Gina mocked and tossed a bag of Twinkies off to the side.

"Don't listen to Gina," Anya reassured her. "We're proud of you. Maybe you'll cure cancer one day."

Wouldn't that be something. The thought was soothing; Margo's confidence in her future always made her feel calm and peaceful. Still, she wanted to confide in the girls about her morning meeting with Eddie's dad. She pondered it for a moment, but the vibe just wasn't serious enough; the girls debated their weights, the grease factor in the cafeteria pizza, and an upcoming Men on Campus calendar.

Anya spoke between bites of Cheetos, the crumbs clashing with her rose lipstick. "What about Eddie Sullivan or Don Gordon for the calendar cover boys? They're both gorgeous."

"Why don't you ask Margo?" Gina suggested. "She's Eddie's history tutor. Tell us, is Eddie Sullivan as good looking up close as he is from far away—on the basketball court? Running up and down the court in those tight black shorts?"

"Well, he's not going to have time to pose for the calendar if he doesn't make it through class," Margo said lightly.

She tried to get Eddie and the meeting with his dad out of her head by going through her day's agenda. But it was no use. Her mind raced with panic for Eddie and his seemingly hopeless academic career.

Am I the only one who believes in him?

* * *

Eddie sat at the counter of the student lounge nursing a black coffee. Only a few students remained, thankfully, none of his friends. He had a reputation to uphold — that nothing mattered to him, nothing made him sweat— but at this moment, he was sweating. He looked up as Margo came through the door.

Rising from his stool, he called to her. "Hey! Let's grab that table in the corner." He nodded toward an empty table near a window.

Margo met him there, and slid onto a seat, setting her book bag down on the chair next to her. "I'm sorry about this morning. I had no idea what your dad was like."

"Yeah, I should've warned you I had a real fun-loving father," he apologized, and pushed his chair backwards so that it rested on only two legs. "At least he didn't draw blood." He let the chair drop with a bang.

Margo leaned forward over the table, gazing intently at him. "So, let's say you and I work our butts off to prove him wrong."

"Sounds like a plan. Only my Civil War paper is due tomorrow and you know I haven't done shit."

"I've got you covered." Margo pulled a manila folder from her canvas bag and passed it across the table. "Let's just call it an early Christmas present."

He opened the folder and examined a five-page paper on Gettysburg. "You wrote my paper for me?" he wondered. "I thought you had morals. I'm surprised at you."

She was surprised at herself, too. Mostly for falling into the same carefully laid trap as all the other tutors who'd preceded her. "I don't want a broken nose on my conscience if you don't pass history, so I'm willing to strike a deal."

"I'm listening," Eddie perked up.

"I wrote your paper. Now it's up to you to get an A or B on the final. That means you study your ass off and focus on nailing the exam. Deal?"

"Deal." Eddie stuck out his hand and Margo shook it.

"Good," Margo confirmed. She nodded toward the coffee machine. "We're going to need two big cups of coffee and lots of refills. So, go fetch, then tell me everything you know about the Gettysburg Address."

* * *

Three weeks to the day after she'd witnessed the hell Eddie endured from his father, Margo and Eddie met with Professor Turner again. This time she felt confident that Eddie's academic future showed an upward trend. He appeared to be an eager, willing student. They had been burning the midnight oil almost every night.

Professor Turner sat behind her desk and removed her glasses as she eyed Eddie's file. "I'll be direct. I've heard grumblings that a group of athletes scored an A on Father Duggan's history exam."

Margo responded before Eddie had a chance to speak. "Why would anyone complain about students getting an A on the exam?"

"Father Duggan suspects that the test answers may have been stolen from his room," Professor Turner replied in a steely tone. "He can't prove it, and we hope it's not true, but that's the theory. I just wanted to know how you," she directed her stern gaze at Eddie, "feel about getting an A coming on the heels of almost flunking the class?"

Eddie looked at his feet and twisted in his chair.

"Wait a minute, Professor Turner," Margo interjected indignantly. "Eddie killed himself for this test. We had an agreement, and I know he studied. Are you accusing him of cheating?"

"I'm not accusing anyone of anything. I'm just checking to make sure this exam was above-board for Eddie Sullivan. Your thoughts?" she inquired, narrowing her eyes.

"I studied," he stated flatly.

Turner's phone began to ring.

"Good enough, then. This meeting's over." Turner picked up her phone and motioned them to leave with a swift wave of her hand.

"That was really weird," Margo remarked, when she and Eddie were out in the hallway. "I can't believe she would come out and accuse you like that." She swung her book bag over her shoulder. "I'm heading to my biology lab. I'll see you later."

"I'm headed in that direction too. I'll walk you," Eddie offered.

At 10:00 AM, under the bright blue sky, the mid-morning sun glistened off the buildings. Students filled the paths heading toward their various classes, swinging their book bags and clutching apples, milk cartons, or coffee cups.

A freshman stopped Eddie for an autograph. As he signed the girl's notebook, he turned to Margo, "You're coming to tonight's game, right?"

"I wasn't planning on it." Margo replied.

"Come with one of your roommates. I'll leave two tickets at the Arena Center visitor's booth. The game starts at seven sharp. We're the underdog, but everybody loves an underdog."

Margo had learned enough about Eddie over the last couple of weeks to recognize bravado when she witnessed it. This game obviously meant a lot to him. She sensed the undercurrent of pressure he felt.

"Okay, Eddie," she answered. "I'll be there."

He flashed one of his dazzling smiles at her and Margo thought he almost seemed relieved when she agreed to go. *Was it really so important to him?* She stopped at the end of the path leading to the science lab.

"This is me. I guess I'll see you tonight?"

"Cool. Win or lose, the team is having a party at Dempsey's afterward. Meet me there. You can be my date," Eddie said.

"Wow. Thanks."

"And don't forget to hold my lucky charm," Eddie said.

Margo pulled the ring from her front jean pocket. "It's with me all the time."

* * *

Gina lay mostly naked on her side like a burlesque goddess, while Carlos's little group of wannabe artists set up their easels around her. A white sheet draped strategically over her groin and one arm casually covered her breasts. She'd posed for this group before. They were mostly college students willing to pay for some extra tutoring on the side from one of the art school's best and brightest.

She watched Carlos direct his class as he demonstrated technique with his own canvas and paint brushes. She blew him a playful kiss, momentarily revealing her breasts, and basking in the gratifying response from the male class members.

The students were hushed and almost reverent as they

sketched her. The studio's atmosphere was in sharp contrast to the boisterous pep rally Gina had just come from. She shifted her position slightly and scratched her nose, trying to keep her mind quiet, but she the basketball game preoccupied her thoughts. All the girls on her floor were going. It would be televised. The cheerleaders were going to perform on TV!

If I could just be in two places at once.

She focused on remaining frozen so the students wouldn't miss a curve or crevice.

* * *

Margo and Amy waited for the bus to the city with sixty or seventy other excited students. The coeds jostled and joked with each other as they passed more than one bottle of beer surreptitiously around the assemblage. The girls, among the first to board the bus when it arrived, sat in front where they could see the busy streets of downtown Providence through the windshield, as the bus made its way to the downtown sports arena.

First off the parked vehicle, Amy and Margo made a beeline to the box office where their tickets were waiting—not quite front row seats, but close to the Providence home basket, and only three rows back. They took in the sounds of the rapidly filling stadium. The squeak of athletic shoes on the boards and the rhythmic dribbling of multiple basketballs almost drowned out the voices of the boisterous crowd as the teams warmed up.

Reaching their seats, the girls remained standing for a while, their nervous energy not allowing them to simply sit and wait for the game to begin.

"There's Eddie," Margo pointed, just as he received a pass for a warmup shot.

The referee blew the whistle and the game began. The teams traded baskets for the first three quarters. The score was close. At the end of the fourth quarter, with five seconds on the clock, Margo watched Eddie leap up to grab the ball and throw a high-looping pass to his teammate, Doug, who raced toward the opposite end of the court. Doug caught the ball, and shot toward the basket for what should've been an easy lay-up, but one of the opposing players had kept up with him: step for step, and as the shot sailed up, he swatted it away. The ball landed in the hands of CHP's power forward, who dribbled twice and lofted it toward the basket. It arced over the rim just as Eddie jumped into the air, nabbed the ball, and dunked it through the hoop to win the game.

The Christopher Hayes fans leapt to their feet in unison, cheering at the top of their lungs. Caught up in the frenzy, Margo and Amy clapped wildly, shouting for Eddie.

Amy turned to Margo, "Looks like your history student doesn't need any help on the court."

"If only he studied the way he dribbles," Margo laughed.

Amy turned to her, beaming. "Time to party," she giggled.

* * *

It was 11:00 PM when the last student left Carlos's private studio—which was the living room of his two-story apartment. Now fully naked, Gina stood and stretched out her stiff muscles. Even though they were alone, Carlos draped a blue silk bathrobe over her shoulders, as if protecting her modesty.

"That was a good session," Carlos complimented her, lighting a cigarette. "But you seemed out of it, like you weren't really there. What gives?"

"It's not a bug out. Don't worry," she assured him, and rested her head on his shoulder. "It's just that CHP played its big game tonight at the Arena Center."

"So what?" Carlos asked.

"We missed an important basketball game … but we can catch the after party. Come to Dempsey's with me," Gina begged.

"I'm getting too old for Dempsey's. Besides, I had gum stuck on the bottom of my loafers for weeks the last time I went in there."

She made a pouty face. He laughed and gave her a hug. "All right, witch. You go ahead. I'll meet you there."

Gina covered her disappointment with a smile. She knew that tone. "You know you won't meet me there."

He shrugged. "You'll find some other worthy suitor to escort you. There's the phone. Make some young stud's night."

Gina pulled away from him. "That's cruel."

"The idea of 'we' feels a little cruel right now. I don't want a studio girlfriend. I want a full-time one."

"Carlos, I'm eighteen. I'm still in high school. I can't be anyone's full-time anything. Don't you understand?"

"Don't worry. You've made yourself really clear."

"I don't need this hassle. If I wanted someone being a drag on me, I would've moved home and given the job to my parents."

"You need your freedom. Freedom's good."

Carlos stubbed his cigarette out in a dab of red paint on his palette. Then, he walked across the room to where Gina's clothes were strewn on a chair and tossed them to her. "Enjoy your freedom."

"What a lousy deal," Gina whispered despondently. "I get my freedom, but I don't get you."

* * *

The party inside Dempsey's Diner was already going strong when Margo and Amy arrived. Amy stayed outside to chat with friends, while Margo dove into the crowd inside. Her eyes remained fixed on Eddie as she shouldered her way through the crowd.

"Hi," he yelled over the chaos. "C'mon over."

"What a win!" Margo kissed him on the cheek.

He nodded toward the corner end of the counter next to the jukebox. "It's hard to talk. Let's go out to the back porch."

The porch was several decibels quieter. "I didn't even know this was out here," Margo observed, relieved not to have to shout over the music.

"Not many people do," Eddie replied. "It's my private little lair."

The vague scent of marijuana enveloped Margo. She noticed a little wicker sofa with sunflower cushions on the far side of the porch.

"Have a seat," he gestured with one hand, then pulled a joint from his warm-up jacket pocket, lit it, inhaled deeply, then passed it to Margo.

"I don't smoke."

"You didn't do a lot of things before I came along. Hell, you still had your virginity before you met me. I'm a bad influence on you, Doctor Tracey. I suggest you run far and fast."

"Don't think the thought hasn't crossed my mind," Margo warned, laughing.

"I know. An uber-jock and a serious student aren't exactly a match made in heaven. Is that what you were thinking?"

"Pretty much." She looked away.

"That's your problem. You think too much."

"Yeah?" She took the joint from his fingers, inhaled deeply and coughed. "Okay, Sullivan, I'll stop thinking, but just for tonight."

He pushed her down on the love seat and lifted her legs and climbed half on top of her. His hand moved up her halter top with incredible agility, stroking her stomach while he kissed her neck with each stroke of his hand. Instinctively, Margo arched her back while Eddie unzipped her jeans, gliding them and her panties down her legs and onto the concrete floor.

Eddie produced a condom packet and waved it at her. "A little help, miss?"

She laughed. He was always way ahead of her.

"What if someone comes out here?"

"They won't. Trust me."

"I trust you," she told him.

In the aftermath of their private celebration, Eddie sat up with a groan. Margo lay back with her arms over her head, staring into semi-darkness, the air cool on her breasts.

"We're not just celebrating your win on the court, you know."

"What else?" Eddie asked.

"Your win off the court. I'm so proud of your A on your history test. I knew you could do it."

"We better get dressed," Eddie said curtly.

That wasn't the reaction she'd expected. She got up and pulled on her jeans.

Once they were back inside the diner, there was a surge at the door and the bouncer entered, his arms burdened with an oversized sheet cake with each player's number in black icing. Amy and the cheerleaders flocked to Eddie.

"Let's go, Sullivan," the bouncer directed. "Free soda and cake on the house tonight."

Margo helped Amy cut and pass out the cake. Everyone in Dempsey's flocked around them, clamoring for a piece and congratulating Eddie.

When it looked like all the others were occupied eating, Eddie took Margo by the hand and whispered in her ear, "This is a perfect time for us to get lost."

They reached the front door of the bar when Doug blocked the way. "The night is still young, kiddies."

"We'll be back," Eddie explained. "Just getting some air."

Doug winked at Margo. "Hey Margo, what d'you think of your pet project, here? I think we have a chance of making it this year. Maybe all the way to the championship."

"It was a great game," Margo agreed.

Joe, the back-up point guard standing next to them, chimed in. "Did you see Sullivan's face when he nailed the winning shot?"

Doug replied, "Yeah. I've seen that same bewildered look on his face in history class."

"Unbelievable," Joe continued. "Sullivan, what were you more shocked at ... your shot tonight, or the look on Duggan's face when we all scored A's on his test? I mean, you're almost as good at lock-picking as you are at banging the back boards."

Margo turned and tried to slow her breath as she watched the panic flood into Eddie's eyes. He gently nudged her toward the front door.

"Don't listen to Joe. He's high. Too much grass can fry what little brain cells he's got left in there." He gave Joe a more-than-playful slap upside the head.

Margo felt chills all the way down to the center of her soul. "Don't bother lying, again, Eddie. And remember before, when you suggested I run as fast as I can from you? Watch me. "

"What do you mean?" Eddie asked.

"I quit. I am no longer your tutor. No longer your ... whatever it is I am to you. And most of all, no longer your good luck charm." She yanked his ring from her pocket and handed it back.

"You can't quit me." Eddie's voice quivered.

"You're the one that quit."

* * *

Eddie watched Margo storm out Dempsey's front door without looking back.

What the hell, he thought. *Who needs this aggravation? Especially from a girl.*

He looked around the diner. With each glance, a student beamed at him, raising a glass in congratulations. He winked back. A casual wave. He watched Gina walk in with some students and join Amy at the front of the room. This was a celebration. People having fun. Not being hassled. He didn't feel like being hassled.

Screw that.

Even if it killed him (and he thought the feeling he had right now just might), he wasn't going to let it show.

Screw that.

4

Summer: 1977

MARGO STOOD PROUDLY IN the Hawk and finished counting the money in the register. She was more than ready to handle the lunch crowd that would soon be drifting into her family's restaurant. After placing the ketchup bottles and ashtrays on the small tables and sweeping out the booths, she called to the waitress in the back.

"I'll be back later. I'm going to the harbor for the christening of the new Rum Runner boat. I've gotta run or I'll be late."

She hustled out the door and took her usual route to the harbor. Newport's Fourth of July traditions were her favorite parts of the summer. Tourists lined the streets dressed in red, white and blue. The children carried flags in anticipation of the annual parade that preceded the night's fireworks. Margo's colorful sailor shirt and white Bermuda shorts blended in with the patriotic mood.

Waiting for the light on Main Street to turn green, she waved to the street vendors who sold cotton candy, balloons, kites, and pinwheels. She continued down the cobblestone path and stopped in front of the Blue Shell, the town's landmark harbor restaurant, famous for clam chowder and lobster bake. On the outdoor patio, waiters busied themselves placing linens and silverware on the dozen outside round tables. A bartender stood behind the outdoor oyster bar stacking pilsner glasses in a tidy row. The bar-back lifted a tub of iced oysters into its place. When he straightened up and turned around Margo felt like she had been punched in the stomach.

"Hey ex-tutor, want a lemonade?" Eddie yelled. "Haven't seen you since our divorce."

"No thanks." Margo would never dream of accepting anything from Eddie Sullivan. "I'm surprised to see you. What are you doing in Newport?"

Eddie crossed the patio and stood in front of her, wiping his hands on a towel he pulled from his apron. "I'm working the oyster bar at the Shell for the summer."

"Why aren't you home in Boston?"

"I'm spending the summer at a house on Viking Road with some of the players, so I can do summer school. I drive from Newport to CHP every day."

"Then I guess we'll be seeing a lot of each other," Margo sputtered, despite the tightness in her throat.

"Maybe you could tutor me in biology?" Eddie winked.

"No thanks ... been there, done that."

The bartender waved to Margo. "I just saw your dad. I hear you have the honor of christening the new boat." He turned to Eddie and gestured with a wave of his hand. "Why don't you join Margo for an hour before we open for lunch?"

"Sure," Eddie said.

Margo smiled, fuming on the inside. The two walked down

the cobblestone street to the harbor where the crew and passengers stood on the new boat while the captain—Ray Houseman—remained on the dock greeting guests.

"We've been waiting for you to handle the honors," Ray announced, when Margo reached him.

Margo realized everybody's eyes were on her. She glanced up at the guests on the boat; several members of the staff from the Hawk surrounded her father, Gyp. She saw her "date," Ted, standing near the starboard gunwale, and waved at him. Ted, a CHP medical track junior from Providence, spent the summers in Narragansett. They'd been friends from the beginning of their junior year, partnering on different biology projects or meeting up to cram for exams.

She'd invited Ted to the christening on the spur of the moment, when he'd stopped into the Hawk to deliver an invoice for a lobster order the Tracey's placed with his family's fishing business. He caught Margo and her mom mopping the floor. The invitation had been more of a knee-jerk reaction to give her mother some proof that she wasn't so focused on school that she couldn't enjoy an afternoon out with a fellow student.

She ought to be glad she'd done it, so Eddie would see she wasn't pining for him. But, suddenly as she watched Ted adjust his oversized sunglasses while he delicately sipped a bottle of Dr. Pepper, she had second thoughts. His freshly pressed long-sleeved pink button down shirt, madras shorts, and white boat shoes seemed so boring.

She glanced at Eddie. His unruly blonde curls stood straight up and sideways. Barefoot, his tan body stripped to the waist, his muscles rippled with the slightest movement.

He caught her glance. "Who's the guy up on the boat waving to you?"

"My—" She hesitated. "Ted Hart. He's a rising junior at CHP. You don't know him?"

Eddie shook his head. "It doesn't even ring a bell."

"I suppose it wouldn't. If he can't dunk a ball, he might as well be invisible."

Before Eddie could react, Captain Houseman handed Margo an ice-cold bottle of champagne, turned to the crew and passengers on the boat, and spoke. "Thank you, everyone, for coming. We are here to christen our new Rum Runner harbor cruise boat, the *Thomas Tew*, named after Newport's famous pirate. Anyone from this area knows the story and legacy of Newport's very own pirate. But for those of you unfamiliar with the legend, Margo Tracey, our Tour Guide, has the honors."

Margo smiled up at the boatload of guests. "Hi, everybody! Welcome. As Cap Houseman said, Thomas Tew was such a fixture in these parts, he became known as the Rhode Island Pirate. As an Englishman who started his career in the 17th-century as a privateer, he turned to piracy when he found it more lucrative. But Tew only embarked on two voyages before he met a bloody death on the high seas. He's also known for pioneering a route that became known as the Pirate Round. Many other infamous scoundrels followed in his wake, like Henry Every and William Kidd. If you're interested in reading about old Thomas, you can find his story in Captain Charles Johnson's *A General History of the Pyrates*." She pronounced it "pie-rates" and got a laugh.

"The good captain's book is a mash of history and fiction and it's hard to tell which is which. But in christening this boat, I'd like to quote Captain Johnson, who said, 'Tew, in Point of Gallantry, was inferior to none.' I christen thee, *Thomas Tew*."

Margo hoisted the champagne bottle and swung it at the bow. The bottom exploded, causing shattered glass to slice into the water. The guests applauded while Margo, Eddie, and the captain climbed up the gangway and joined the passengers who drank and nibbled on appetizers.

Margo strolled the deck from bow to stern, making sure all of the boat's metal shined with perfect polish. The deck looked immaculate. The newly varnished mahogany rails shone beautifully.

After a loud click, the captain's voice came across the boat's speaker system. "Ladies and gentlemen, enjoy yourselves as we take the *Thomas Tew* for her maiden run around the harbor."

Amid cheers and applause, he revved the engine, steered the boat out of the congested harbor, and headed toward the bridge, chugging past fishermen with their rods hanging from the upscale charter boats. The party rolled on.

Margo found her father in the crowd on the foredeck, and watched him order another drink. She pretended not to be counting, but she couldn't help herself; old habits die hard. It was barely noon, and he already looked tipsy.

She joined her date, Ted, who kissed her on the cheek and whispered, "Thanks for inviting me."

He passed her a bottle of Perrier and they toasted to Newport and to *Thomas Tew*. They talked for some time about biochemistry and their last lab report on the colonization of proteins. Just as she was beginning to relax, Eddie ambled over with a paper plate loaded with finger food. He extended his free hand to Ted and gave him a commanding shake.

Then he turned to Margo. "Boy, your father really knows how to have a good time. I guess you must take after your mother. Is she the serious one?"

Margo bristled at Eddie's comments. Having a good time wasn't how she'd describe watching her father stumble around the guests, slapping them on their backs spilling beer as he spoke. Her father's drinking embarrassed Margo, because with each beer he grew louder and more foolish.

She turned her attention back to Ted, who was listening to Eddie brag about himself and his plans to lead CHP to the All-State High School finals in the winter, as well as train the younger players to carry on his hoops legacy.

Terribly fascinating, Margo thought. *If only he could add and subtract.*

"Don't you think the captain should bring us back? It's been over an hour," Margo remarked.

"Relax, Doctor Tracey. Enjoy the sun and fun." Eddie chugged the beer he'd sneaked from the bar and wiped his mouth with the back of his hand.

"Hey, I'll get you another drink." Ted, suddenly a lovesick child enamored with Eddie's athletic *bona fides*, left for the bar.

"Quite the guy," Eddie commented.

"I wouldn't know. Is he your date, or mine?"

The captain spoke again. "We're getting ready to head back to the harbor so this is last call for the bar."

That caused a run on the bar, of course. Margo shook her head. Poor Ted was probably getting trampled.

Eddie gestured at Margo's dad, leaning over the rail, laughing as salt spray hit his face. "Your dad sure likes the sea air."

"Not as much as he likes booze," Margo muttered.

The boat bobbled in sync with the choppy waves. A hard breeze whipped up the swells as Captain Houseman brought the craft around and pointed her toward shore. Margo heard her father's voice yelling above the sound of wind, waves, and chatter.

"We used to do this in the Navy!"

Oh, just shoot me, Margo thought, then reluctantly turned to look. Gyp teetered precariously on the bottom rail, leaning out over the side of the boat.

"Catch a wave!" he shouted, throwing his arms wide.

A rogue wave broke over the starboard bow, undermining Gyp's tenuous foothold. His feet slipped, and the receding wave carried him overboard. He slid between the rail and the gunwale, momentarily hidden from view in the rough chop.

Margo screamed.

Eddie acted. Kicking off his shoes, he followed Gyp into the cold waters of the bay. Margo unfroze herself and dashed to the starboard rail, where she became a helpless bystander. When Eddie's head broke the water's surface, he rapidly surveyed the area and located the older man foundering in the whitecaps. Stroking powerfully, he reached Gyp, whose thrashing arms threatened to drown them both.

"Turn onto your back!" Eddie shouted. "I've got you." He skillfully maneuvered Gyp into a lifeguard's hold and began side-stroking toward the nearest of the life preserver rings the crew had tossed into the harbor.

The captain had brought the *Thomas Tew* to a full stop, and passengers and crew watched anxiously as Eddie guided Gyp toward the boat. Two crew members hastily mounted a ladder over the side, and helped the soaking men out of the water and onto the deck, where Gyp lay gasping and trembling from exhaustion. Eddie stood doubled over, hands on his knees, gulping in deep breaths.

Margo knelt, watching over her father as his breathing stabilized. Looking up at Eddie, she felt a wave of gratitude wash over her, along with a feeling of uncomfortable ambivalence.

"You're on," she declared, shielding her eyes with one hand.

"On for what?" Eddie gasped, still trying to catch his breath.

"Summer school and biology—I'll tutor you. Meet me at the Newport Library Monday at eleven. And don't you dare stand me up."

5

A FEW WEEKS HAD PASSED since Margo had resurrected her studies with Eddie. At nearly 11:00 AM, she reached the entrance to the Newport Public Library, an old brownstone converted to community service. The sun beamed over the crowded village streets, flashing off the long rows of shading maples adorned with leaves sparkling like green sequins.

Inside the building, Margo scanned for Eddie, who'd promised he'd be there early. She spied him bent over the water fountain in the corner. He turned and waved. They met at a small table next to the copy machine.

"You look surprised to see me," he remarked. "What's the matter, you didn't think I'd show?"

"I knew you'd be here," Margo lied, as she sat down and placed her biology books on the scratched table. "I'm just surprised you actually brought books with you and something to write with."

Eddie frowned. "Hey, I've shown up every day for the last month. When are you gonna cut me a break? I'm doing my time."

Margo laughed at his exaggerated affront. "Didn't realize time with me was a prison sentence. I'll admit it—you're serious this time."

"Yeah, I am," Eddie replied. "What do you want from me? Do I have to sign a contract in blood?"

"A little blood would be nice, now that you mention it. Or, you know, actually being nice. Why do you always have to talk to me like such a wise ass?"

"Maybe because I am a wise ass?" Eddie retorted.

She raised her hands in surrender. "I give up. Let's get down to some plant reproduction."

He grinned. "You mean plants having drunken sex? I love it when you talk dirty."

"You really crack yourself up, don't you?" Margo tried to act annoyed, but couldn't help laughing. "Turn to page five—we can start with orchids."

A few hours later, stepping out of the dim recesses of the library, they blinked as their eyes adjusted to the late afternoon sun. They strolled up Main Street, paused at a hot dog vendor set up near the front doors called out, "Can I interest you in some lunch?"

"Sure," they answered in unison. Waiting in front of the cart, they watched the vendor expertly extract two hot dogs from the steaming water and insert them into fresh buns, piling on heaps of sauerkraut and icing them with yellow mustard.

They continued west on Main Street until they reached the turnoff for the cliff walk. There they joined the slow-moving procession of tourists who'd been drawn to this famous prome-nade of stony beach cliffs and century-old mansions. After only a few yards, they stopped and leaned over the balustrade to take in the view: fifty feet below, waves swept into every crevice and pounded the rocks before reluctantly drawing back, leaving foam in their wake.

They meandered farther and Margo pointed out and gave a mini-history lesson on some of the mansions situated on the other side of the walkway. Midway along the cliff walk, a set of steep stairs descended to an overlook only ten feet above the rocky coastline. Single file, they gingerly stepped down to the lower scenic view. Spray from the biggest waves splashed their faces and dampened their clothes and knapsacks.

They placed their satchels at the foot of the stairs and leaned back, resting their elbows on the safety rail. A stiff breeze blew Margo's wavy hair into her face. She brushed it away and tucked it behind her ears.

"Can we talk about something?" she asked.

"Sounds serious. You gonna lecture me about the many methods of cleaning safety goggles for maximum protection from deadly chemicals?"

"We should talk about that, actually, but not today." She chose her words carefully. "When we were working on your plant reproduction presentation, I noticed you reversed your letters in the closing summary."

"What're you talking about?"

"I mean that in many places you wrote an 'N' when you meant to write a 'Y'."

"So, I made some mistakes." Eddie shrugged his shoulders.

"I think it's more than that. I noticed the same thing in your written narrative of key observations. It seemed like a pattern."

"I'm sure it's no big deal."

"I wasn't sure at first. Then I looked at a sequence of sentences you strung together for the key observations of your lab work, and the events are out of order. But only on paper;

verbally, you get everything in the right order." Pulling a notebook out of her book bag, she pointed to a sheet. "Take a look at
the outline you wrote for me. See what I mean?"

Eddie barely glanced at the page. "Okay, so it's no secret I
get a little twisted around. Isn't that why I have a tutor?"

"Like I said, I think it's more than that," Margo explained.
"I've been doing some research and I think you may have this
learning disability I read about called dyslexia."

He scowled. "Oh, now I get it. Doctor Tracey has made her
first human diagnosis. Get tired of prescribing treatment for
worms with heat rash?"

She shook her head vehemently. "No, it's not like that. I'm
worried about you, Eddie. I'd like to talk to Professor Turner
about it tomorrow morning."

"If you're right, this is a sure-fire way to get you what you've
been looking for."

Margo frowned. "What do you mean? I'm trying to help."

"Who are you trying to help—you, or me? You want advancement. If you're right, and you've discovered something, you'll go
down in the tutor's hall of fame. Maybe there will be a statue
of the great Margo Tracey outside the library, standing proud
dangling a lab rat from your upraised fist." He pantomimed the
gesture.

That stung. "I'm sorry, I didn't mean to make you mad."

"It's cool," Eddie deflected, then shifted closer to her.

Not trusting his closeness, Margo sidled away, moving to
hoist herself onto one of the long flat rocks tucked in against
the cliff on the landward side of the walkway. Eddie followed
her, and together, they stared out at the magnificent view of the
ocean before them.

She dangled her feet over the edge of the rock. "So, are you okay with me calling Professor Turner tomorrow morning?"

"That depends."

"On what?" She watched him chuck a small rock over the edge of the bluff.

"What's in it for me? Educational advantages like some kind of dyslexic discount off my biology presentation?"

"This isn't about squeaking by in class so you can play more ball," Margo remarked. "It's about getting more specialized help if you do have a problem. I mean, what happens when you graduate and have to find a job? If you get help now, you can work differently and make adjustments."

"Word on the street says I have a good chance at getting drafted by the NBA."

"What if you're not? Or what if you get injured?"

She knew she had gone too far when she saw the pained look in Eddie's face at the mere mention of any type of injury.

She tried to backtrack. "Let me show you what I mean. Let's go over the opening paragraph of the first page of your presentation." She hopped down from the rock, snatched up her satchel, pulled a folded piece of lined composition paper from the front pocket and passed it to him.

He opened it up and briefly scanned it, while she climbed back up next to him.

"I don't feel like looking at this now." He handed her back the paper, then clutched her hand.

Margo felt the calluses on his hand and the strength of his grip. Her body stirred, but she pulled her hand loose and shifted her position to face the sea, cramming the paper into her pocket. Eddie took her by the shoulders and gently turned her to face him. She kept her eyes down, wondering where this was going.

They'd developed a nice friendship that she didn't want to spoil. At the same time, she couldn't deny the goodbyes at the library's exit grew longer and more flirtatious with every session. But those exchanges were on her turf, under the safe awning of the tutor-student relationship. Now, here, tucked away beneath the cliff's overhang, with the wild waves breaking below, she felt control slipping away.

Eddie caressed her chin in the palm of his hand and moved in for a kiss. "I'm not usually sober when I kiss someone." His body pressed too close.

Margo pulled back a little. "We've gotten to be friends, Eddie. Should we be doing this?"

"I think this is the first time you've got a question and you don't have the answer," he laughed. "Must be scary. I'll admit it; I'm scared, too, 'cause I'm trying to kiss you in broad daylight."

"Maybe it's better if we just stop here." She pulled her legs up and hugged her knees, feeling like a turtle withdrawing into its shell.

Eddie took the signal. He sat back and crossed his arms. "Guess I'll have to get you drunk."

"Not funny."

"Hypnosis? Magic?" He waggled his fingers like a magician getting ready to pull a rabbit out of a hat.

Margo shook her head and suppressed a smile.

Eddie flexed his muscles. "You sure you don't want a piece of this? Look at these guns."

"I'll pass." She hopped off the rock. "Want to keep exploring the rock formations?"

"Go crazy. I need a cold shower." He worked his way to the foot of the steps.

Margo looked out at the waves and let herself remember what it felt like to be in Eddie's arms. Maybe he was right. Maybe keeping things platonic was a mistake.

Maybe. But at least this way, she remained in control.

6

NEWPORT HARBOR COULD GET busy in the summer months, but the Jazz Festival transformed it into a watery version of Times Square. All types of boats, from slow moving sailboats to high speed cigarette racers, crisscrossed the harbor. Gina stood on the sun-drenched dock, taking in the scene. She lowered her sunglasses from the top of her head to the bridge of her nose to cut the 6:00 PM sun glare, as the glowing orb angled toward the horizon.

She searched for the catamaran she and a group of friends had chartered for the day. Normally the craft would be easily visible, but the many vessels floating in the sparkling blue waters, made it difficult to pick out. Then she saw it, sailing toward the dock like a swan on a mission from God.

"Here it comes," shouted Gina.

The ten teenagers lounging behind her on the dock, amid coolers of soda, beer (for those now of legal drinking age) and picnic gear, began to rouse themselves and prepare to board as the catamaran docked. The white, twenty-five foot long boat had a small cabin with a kitchen and toilet, but the passengers would be traveling on the hard fiberglass deck that stretched between the outriggers.

Eddie, Margo, Gina and several of Eddie's basketball teammates and their dates, jumped onto the boat and dumped their gear. Benches covered with blue pillows that doubled as life jackets lined the catamaran's aft gunwales. Most of the girls arranged themselves on the pillows, while the guys sat on the rail with their feet on the seats.

"I can see none of you boys are sailors," shouted the captain, Ralph Gunn, "or you'd know that when a sailboat tacks, the boom swings from one side to the other, and all you fellas sitting up there are going to find yourself in the harbor."

The boys sheepishly jumped down from their precarious perches as Captain Gunn unmoored the boat, using the auxiliary outboard motor to push away from the dock. A sudden gust of wind tightened the sail, hastening their pursuit of the other boats, all heading toward the festival's concert venue. Sailboats zigzagged across the catamaran's path as they approached the amphitheater, then Captain Gunn lowered the sails and employed the auxiliary motor to get as close as they could to the venue. The concert's live radio simulcast complemented their relative proximity to the stage.

The first act took the stage and flooded the open waters with the sounds of saxophone, bass, and drums. Gina scanned the passengers in the boats to either side. She reacted to the scene in front of her as if someone had just dumped ice down her back.

Margo sat down next to her and held out a can of beer. "What are you staring at?" she asked, bewildered.

"It's Carlos. On the catamaran. Right next to us," Gina pointed. Her throat felt tight and she knew her voice sounded strange. "And get an eyeful of the babe in the white bikini lounging next to him."

Gina raised her hand to shade her eyes from the sun's glare. They were about fifteen feet away—close enough that she could tell the woman was Carlos's contemporary. Plus, her olive skin made that damned white bikini practically glow.

"You guys split up before Christmas break. That was six months ago. Why is it bothering you now?" Margo questioned.

"I never thought he'd find someone else. I mean, I guess I considered…" Her voice drifted off.

"You thought he would remain celibate until you graduated?"

"Something like that," Gina replied miserably.

She wasn't prepared for what happened next. Carlos turned and kissed the woman—a long, deep kiss. Gina's blood began to boil. Something inside her snapped. She grabbed Margo's arm.

"Yes, that's Carlos, all right, french-kissing some tacky whore. He doesn't see me yet, but I'm going to get his attention in about two seconds."

"Don't do anything crazy. You were the one who told Carlos to back off and give you some space and, boy, do you have space. You were just telling me five minutes ago how much you *love* the skipper's butt."

"So what?"

"So then, why shouldn't Carlos play the field?"

Gina shook her head. Margo was right. She wanted to have things both ways. She'd given Carlos his freedom, but still enjoyed when he followed her around campus like some lonesome hound dog. She hadn't expected him to taste his freedom so literally.

Margo frowned at her, perplexed, obviously waiting for a response. Gina ignored her. "Yeah, but just look at them—making out all hot and heavy in front of the whole festival. They need to cool it … and I have just the trick."

Gina power-walked the length of the deck and into the cabin. She found what she needed hanging on the wall next to the door—a lovely red fire extinguisher. She carried it back to the bow, lifted it to her shoulder, and released the valve.

"Hey, you artsy-fartsy gigolo!" she shouted.

Carlos and the olive-skinned woman pulled themselves out of each others' longing gazes to stare at Gina.

"Good, I got your attention!" she shouted. "You guys are just too damned hot not to cool down!"

She aimed the nozzle at Carlos's groin and fired. Direct hit. She got him dead center on the front of his bright red Speedo. His reaction exceeded her expectations; he leapt to his feet with a wild yelp, batting foam from his groin.

Gina laughed. "Damn, I'm good!"

"Hey, what are you doing?" Captain Gunn shouted at them from the helm.

"Just putting out a little fire."

"Okay, he got the message," Margo noted, pulling the foamy extinguisher from Gina's hands. "Glad to see you're not the jealous, possessive type."

Margo grabbed Gina's arm and led her to the opposite side of the catamaran to sit down. Gina continued laughing as if the whole scene were not intensely embarrassing. She felt the eyes of the skipper and the other kids on her, but avoided their gazes.

The concert well underway, Margo reached into a cooler, pulled out a root beer, popped the tab, and handed the can to her friend. "Cheers," she toasted. "Let's make the most of it. We're here and the skipper's now flexing his muscles for you."

"You want me to drown my sorrows in root beer?" Gina

asked incredulously. "I'd prefer the real thing." She took a sip anyway, licking at the foam on her upper lip.

"You don't need the real thing. Besides, you've already dowsed a skinny artist in a Speedo. You have another trick up your sleeve?"

Gina shook her head. Her bag of tricks was empty.

* * *

Four hours later, the concert wound down. The sun had long set, but a full moon threw a stark white light over the entire harbor, illuminating the flotilla of bobbing boats. Captain Gunn encouraged the kids to gather all the empty beverage cans and put them in a large black plastic bag.

While the boats had arrived over the course of several hours, most of the captains started their engines and headed home at the same time, creating a bottleneck at the marina's entrance. Well into the night, the catamaran finally docked at the harbor.

"Let's go for drinks at the Fish House," Gina suggested—an idea that met with instant approval.

Margo flashed her a hard look, though. Gina's flushed cheeks and too-bright smile belied the fact that she obviously hadn't gotten over seeing Carlos with someone else.

They strolled along the wharf to the quaint outdoor bar and grill. A white awning supported by decorated poles sheltered a handful of tables, while a musician played acoustic guitar and sang songs of summer romances. The group settled at a table close to the guitar player, just as he broke into a Crosby, Stills and Nash song. His fingers flew over the frets and strings, and the whole place erupted with applause when he finished. When the applause died down, a waitress appeared to take their drink orders.

Margo had meant to get some wine or a beer, but the breeze off the ocean was cooling; instead she ordered coffee.

"So, are you and Eddie back on?" Gina asked her suddenly.

"Where did that come from?" Margo wondered.

"I saw the way you looked at him all day today. And I know you're tutoring him again, this time in bi-o-lo-gy. Don't pretend all you're doing with him is anatomy diagrams. You can't be studying the nervous system for all those hours without doing some testing on sensory input."

"We're just friends," Margo assured her. "But ... I don't know. I don't trust him."

"Just what I thought. Our little doctor is in lo-ove."

"Who said anything about love? I'm not going to let history repeat itself and fall into a relationship with Eddie the way ... the way his other tutors did." *The way I did before.*

"Who mentioned anything about a relationship? I'm talking about getting laid under the stars. You're in Newport; it's summer time. Forget relationships and live it up. Stop trying to prove you're above the rest of us."

"I never implied that," Margo argued. "I'm not above—"

"You don't have to *say* it. The look on your face when Amy and I come in drunk after a night at a kegger says it all."

Margo glanced around the patio, searching for an escape, but Gina stayed two steps ahead of her. "You can't run to the lab and hide this time. Besides, Eddie Sullivan with a tan is too much to take. Take my advice and have some fun."

"Who's having fun?" Eddie reached across the table and grabbed a napkin to wipe at a big spot of something that had spilled all over the front of his t-shirt.

"Me, hopefully," Gina chimed in as she winked at Eddie and left the table for the outdoor bar.

"I hope your wild and crazy roommate isn't a bad influence. I wouldn't want her getting in the way of your quest for the Nobel prize in biology," Eddie added.

Margo finished her coffee and looked at him. "Want to hitch a ride to the cliff walk?"

"Depends."

"I know, it depends on what's in it for you. The thing is, I don't know."

"Then, have a nice time. I'm having fun here."

"I'm so glad you're not the selfish type," Margo got up from the table, closed out her part of the tab with the waitress and made her goodbyes to everyone.

She left the Fish House and strolled to Main Street , her usual spot to hitch a ride. In five minutes a beat up red Chevy pickup pulled over just ahead of her. The driver, who sported a bushy red beard and a painter's cap, leaned over to open the passenger door. She knew him—sort of. He came into the Hawk a lot and sat at the bar watching sports on TV. Everyone called him 'Red'. She had no idea if that was an actual name or just a reference to the color of his facial hair. She smiled and climbed in.

"Where to, home?"

"Cliff walk," she requested.

He dropped her at the trail head and tipped his painter's hat. She thanked him, then realized, after he'd driven off, that the gathering fog was closer to rain. It fell in a fine mist on her face, and the ocean breeze that stirred it brought with it a strong scent of brine. She walked gingerly down the path to the steps leading to the observation deck, then descended the rain-slick steps. Darkness obscured her view, but she could feel, as well as hear, the crash of the waves. Continuing down a narrow walkway to her favorite jumble of rocks, she sat and stared out at the sea, occasionally catching sight of stars when the fog shifted.

Suddenly Margo realized she had company. "How long have you been following me?" she queried.

Eddie stepped before her. "I caught a ride right after you did."

"I'm just here to watch the fog and stars dance," Margo remarked, looking back out at the water, "so, you might get a little bored."

"I'm here for more than star gazing," Eddie replied.

He leaned down so his face was only inches from hers. She could feel his warm breath on her cheek. It would be so easy just to let go—no complications, no thought of consequences ... but there always were consequences.

She stiffened and pulled away. "I don't know," she murmured.

He didn't move off. Instead, he dropped down next to her on the damp rock.

"Now, that's what I like, Margo. Something you don't know."

He reached out and drew her to him, while she had the irrelevant thought that he hardly ever called her by her name. The delirious sensation of his mouth against hers felt natural. Fitting. He pushed her back, until she balanced on her elbows. Then he unbuttoned her shirt, pulled it down over her arms, and reached around to unhook her bra.

It's all happening again! I don't trust you.

Margo pushed his hands away and scooted sideways, pulling her shirt back onto her shoulders. "This has to stop here." She commanded, quietly, but firmly, trying to ignore the heat radiating through her. *It's for the best.*

Eddie sat up with a bewildered expression on his face. When

76

he spoke, his voice held none of its usual flippancy. "Where do we go from here, Margo?"

"I don't know," she wondered. "I just don't know."

* * *

Eddie sat perched on a barstool in the Hawk behind the pool table, watching his buddy, Doug, take his final shot. His forehead was sweaty and his body overheated, even though he wore just a thin grey t-shirt and painter shorts. The dark, paneled walls, heavy red curtains on the windows, and blaring jukebox created a cocoon of sorts, shutting out the sounds of a Saturday night in Newport. It was almost 10:30 PM and he had exhausted the possibilities here: a few rounds of pool and a couple of sodas. The real fun, he knew, would come later that night.

He stood up and, retrieving the balls from the pockets, racked them absent-mindedly, watching Margo as she went about her duties.

He had stopped into the Hawk earlier that day to invite Margo to his late night keg party. But that wasn't his only request. He'd propositioned her to join him in borrowing the *Thomas Tew* for a late night harbor cruise with his friends later in the week. He thought she might be open to something a little adventurous after their close call on the cliff walk. He'd almost had her again, he was sure of it.

His gaze followed her as she placed ketchup bottles in the clean booths. He stood up, set the eight ball in the middle of the pool table, selected a cue from the wall rack, and took the first shot, breaking the balls and sinking one. Then he passed the cue to his roommate, Doug.

"Find a new partner. I'm grabbing a soda."

Striding across the room, Eddie tapped Margo on the shoulder, "Hey, it's almost quittin' time. Can you pull yourself away from the ketchup and talk to me about taking the *Thomas Tew* out for a late night cruise?"

She wiped her hands on a tea towel and put a hand in her apron pocket as if she were considering handing over the keys; he heard their muted jingle as she fingered them. For a moment Eddie thought he'd won, then she shook her head.

"I haven't changed my mind. The answer is still no."

"Where's your adventurous spirit? You can't stay locked in your lab surrounded by protein detectors for the rest of your high school career. Live a little. We'll take out the *Thomas Tew* together."

Margo looked him in the eye. "Water safety rules…"

He tuned her out once she squinted her eyes and started to talk like a Coast Guard officer. So much for thinking she could change and loosen up, the way she had started to the other night. As he pondered listening again, her lecture shifted from water safety to an even more repellent subject: summer school.

"I spoke to Professor Turner this morning. When do you want to sit down and review what we discussed?"

He laughed. "How about after we graduate?"

"Seriously, Eddie. We need to resolve this."

"Sure. What about tonight … after I throw down a six pack of beer? Are you coming to our late-night party?"

"I can't make it. One of the waitresses called in sick, so I have to set up for tomorrow."

"Too bad. Are Gina and Amy still meeting you here?"

"Yeah. Amy came down to spend the weekend with Gina's cousins who live in Jamestown. They told us they'd be here around closing time, which I think is soon. Don't leave without them. They want to follow you guys over to your house. Okay?"

"Sure, I think I see them now, coming through the front door," Eddie said, glancing in that direction.

Margo followed his gaze.

"Good. Gina, we know, will find someone to hang with at the party. I'm not sure about Amy. You better keep an eye on her and make sure she gets home okay."

Eddie waved at Amy and Gina as they made their way to the bar, then put his arm around Margo's waist and squeezed. "I'll make sure Amy is taken care of," he promised.

He watched Amy lift a pop bottle to her lips and toss money on the bar. She looked over her shoulder and smiled at him. He knew from experience when something was going to happen, and every time he saw Amy, he wanted something to happen with her. They'd flirted during the school year when they'd seen each other out, or when he'd bumped into her outside of Francis Hall while he waited for Margo. More than once he'd been tempted to cancel his dreaded study appointments and hang with Amy, but it wasn't worth another beat-down conference with Professor Turner ... or Margo.

His attempts not to stare at Amy failed miserably. To distract himself, Eddie jammed his hand into his pocket to check its contents, and clenched his fingers around the keys to the *Thomas Tew*. Margo might know how to scoop bacteria out of a plate of chemicals or whatever the hell was her life's mission, but it would be a cold day in hell before she found out about Eddie's pick-pocketing skills.

He turned to her with a grin. "I'll let you go back to your

chowder bowls. We'll miss you tonight." He left, while she remained hunched over the booth counting sugar packets.

On his way to the pool table, he detoured to the bar and tapped Amy on the shoulder. "Party at my house. We're leaving in a few minutes." Eddie led the procession out the door; the rest followed.

* * *

The next morning, Margo waited for Gina and Amy in a booth at Spencer's Cafe. They were late. She hoped they wouldn't be too much longer. She planned to meet Eddie at 9:00 AM at the *Thomas Tew*'s slip to talk about the dyslexia tests she and Professor Turner had discussed yesterday morning by telephone. Finally, the girls appeared at the restaurant entrance, looking a little the worse for wear. Pulling off their sunglasses, they slid into the booth on the bench facing Margo.

"Sorry to keep you waiting," Gina apologized, blinking reddened eyes. "Neither of us got a lot of sleep last night."

"That's okay. How was the party?" Margo asked.

"I hooked up with Doug," Gina blurted out. "We went skinny dipping with a bunch of the guests after the cruise."

"Sounds romantic," Margo laughed.

The waitress arrived and pulled a pencil from her bun.

"I already ordered," Margo remarked. "You guys go ahead."

After the girls placed their orders, Amy started playing with the salt and pepper shakers and relating all the gory details about Eddie's late night party. "It was so amazing. Too bad you had to work."

"Looks like I missed a lot of excitement." She looked at Gina, who was busy emptying packs of sugar into her coffee. "So you went skinny dipping after the cruise. I'm confused. What cruise are you talking about?"

"Go ahead, Gina, tell her how much fun the cruise was."

"Yes, tell me. Don't leave anything out," Margo insisted.

"Well," Gina began. "Eddie took everyone out on the *Thomas Tew*. You know, the boat you sometimes work on."

"Everyone?" Margo asked.

"Yup, but most of us left around two AM. Some of us stayed on board," Gina winked at Amy.

"You know what? I'm absolutely famished!" Amy exclaimed.

"Of course you're starving," Gina concurred. "You worked so hard last night."

Margo glanced from Gina to Amy. "Can I get in on the joke?"

"Sure," Gina explained. "Let's just say you christened the boat in the beginning of the summer, and Amy and Eddie re-christened it last night."

"It was so romantic," Amy smiled. "After we dropped everyone off at the harbor, Eddie snuck into the Blue Shell and filled a cooler with beers. Then, just the two of us went back on the boat for a private moonlight cruise."

Margo toyed with a napkin, not daring to look at Amy. She fought the increasing urge to gouge Amy's eyes out of her silly head.

"We counted the stars and talked about poetry," Amy continued dreamily.

Gina laughed. "Eddie Sullivan reciting poetry. I'd like to hear that."

"Oh, yeah, I can imagine his poem right now," Margo drawled in a voice dripping with sarcasm. "No doubt something about the scent and texture of a basketball."

She hoped the two girls couldn't hear the wild thumping of her heart. Eddie would stop at nothing to get what he wanted and he clearly desired Amy, not her. She'd been right not to trust him. If she'd given in to him the other night... She felt scalded.

She slid out of the booth and threw three dollar bills on the table. "I better get going."

"But you haven't got your food yet," Gina protested.

"Yeah, and we need to talk about our dorm room for next semester. I thought we were going to flip a coin to see who got the single bed," Amy remembered.

"Maybe we shouldn't make any changes since last year brought us good luck," Gina suggested.

"Fine by me," Margo replied, a little curtly. She'd had enough of good luck charms and all that other superstitious nonsense. "I'm late for an appointment."

Margo walked brusquely through town to the harbor side slip where the *Thomas Tew* remained moored. She felt a sharp pang of disgust as she stepped on the boat. Up until today, she'd felt pride every time she climbed aboard the pristine boat. Now, thinking about Eddie and Amy and what must have gone on last night, her anger flared.

She made a beeline for the utility closet below decks to retrieve a mop, a bottle of cleanser, and a pail from the clutter of cleaning fluids and tools, and went to work scrubbing the deck clean. With each forceful push of the mop, she attempted to banish any evidence of Eddie's sexual indiscretions. While she thrust the mop fast and furiously, she heard footsteps on the dock.

"Do you do windows?" Eddie, holding a donut and a can of soda, inquired. "I think you missed a spot," he observed, pointing to a strip along the port rail.

She pivoted around, the mop still in her right hand. "What do you want?"

"You asked me to meet you here at nine to talk about your call with Professor Turner. So, I'm here, hung over as hell, but I'm here."

"I have nothing to say to you. I resign from my tutoring assignment. Maybe I should move on to the ice hockey students. They're probably less trouble," Margo spit out.

"You're not really officially my tutor anymore anyway. But, have it your way. What did I do this time?"

"How was your moonlight cruise on the *Tew* last night? Don't try slipping the boat keys back in my pocket. Just give them to me now." She held her hand out.

Eddie fished the keys out of his jeans and placed them in her palm. She ignored the tingling sensation when her skin met his.

"Amy gets lost going from the cafeteria to our dorm room, so you found yourself a real stimulating girlfriend." She hurled the mop across the deck.

"It was one night on a boat—no strings attached. Relax," Eddie placated her. "Besides, you were the one, not me, who mentioned that night on the cliff walk you didn't know where things stood. I'm guessing you're still not sure."

"Yeah," Margo confirmed. She wanted to tell him she had missed him terribly since they'd been an 'item.' She longed to share her feelings for him and how she couldn't allow herself to let him in. Instead, she rationalized, "If you count up all the facts, we just have too many things working against us."

"Yeah. Right. Too many *things*," Eddie counted. "Look at all these things that just don't work—like this place. I mean, this far out Newport atmosphere, all the good times we have together. Our chemistry. Or is it biology? Why don't you lay it on me—the truth—this is all about that test, isn't it?"

"That's part of it, but other obstacles are getting in the way … my grades slipped before Christmas break. It took me all of second semester to get back to straight A's. "

Eddie put his hand up. "Let me stop you there. You gave me all of your facts. What about your feelings? How do you *feel* about me?"

She took a deep breath. *I don't trust you. Tell me why I should.* "I need time."

Eddie laughed. "Well, that's the one thing we got going for us. Lots and lots of time."

"Professor Turner wants to meet with you and a few members of the English faculty to see if they can arrange some testing for you before we head back to school."

"Why are you changing the subject?" Eddie asked.

Margo looked away. The harbor scene blurred into a hazy watercolor.

"Have it your way," Eddie sighed, then: "Maybe we should take the boat out, and say goodbye to the summer. As friends."

"You're sober. I thought you didn't do crazy things unless your bloodstream was loaded with alcohol," Margo egged him on.

"I know, so help me get the boat out before I lose my nerve."

He deftly moved to the bow and cast off, then turned to look at Margo. She stared at him for a long moment, then moved to coil the ropes. Eddie grabbed a pole and pushed the *Thomas Tew* away from its mooring, while Margo turned over the engine. The mid-morning sun glistened on the wavelets of the bay and seagulls swooped and circled the boat, calling to each other as they searched for food. The forward momentum of the boat provided the only breeze.

Eddie stood beside Margo at the helm, pointing out the ring of seagulls round the lighthouse. "Let's get a closer look," he invited.

They continued west until they came upon the jutting rocks that supported the lighthouse, which stood on the far side of the Newport bridge. Margo throttled back the engines, but misjudged their position. They both cringed at the sound of the rocks scraping the hull. She cut the engine while Eddie moved to drop the anchor. Slipping over the gunwale, he leapt to a large rock to inspect the damage.

Margo gasped as she noted in horror that the rocks had scraped the paint off the entire port side of the *Tew*.

"It's nothing," Eddie knelt down and ran his fingers across the scratched and peeling paint.

"Get back in, "Margo's voice cracked. "We've gotta get this fixed right away."

"Think about it," Eddie reasoned. "We can panic and rush back to the harbor and get ourselves in trouble or we can climb to the lighthouse landing first." He took her hand. "Come on, we're going to get into trouble anyway. Let's postpone the inevitable."

Postpone the inevitable, Margo thought. Eddie's motto, apparently. But looking down at his hand holding hers, feeling his gentle but strong grip, she felt herself weaken.

"Okay," she agreed, hesitantly. "But only for a little while. Then we have to get back."

They clambered over the rocks and up the steep slope to the door at the base of the old lighthouse. A hand-written sign on the door read, "Went to town. Back at two o'clock."

Eddie tried the door, which swung open easily. "Anybody here?" he called.

His voice echoed off the walls of the ancient building. No reply. They ascended the winding wrought iron staircase to the enclosed observation deck, which had a wooden floor and wrap-around windows. Above their heads the huge rotating lamp at the top of the lighthouse rested, as if ready to send its beacon of light out into the sea. They crossed to the far side of the deck where an old wooden door opened onto the living quarters.

Standing inside the small square space, they peered around to see a neatly made cot, a maple desk covered in nautical charts, and a row of hooks hung with yellow rain slickers and flashlights. On the floor a pair of fisherman's boots waited to be put to work.

"Sit down and make yourself comfortable." Eddie gestured to the cot.

"This is the lighthouse keeper's quarters. I don't think we're supposed to be in here."

"I know. That's what makes it exciting." He moved in close to her, his hands encircling her waist. "We could do it your way—leave here the way we came, as friends who had some fun together, or we could say goodbye to Newport with our clothes off. Let's face it, next week, we'll be back on campus. I'll be in the gym most of the time and you'll go back into your science caves."

Margo shook her head. "This year's going to be different for you. Professor Turner registered you with the state for the dyslexia testing."

Eddie rolled his eyes. "That's a sure-fire way to kill my mood—talking about Professor Turner."

He unhitched the clasps of her overalls. The bib fell to her waist exposing a green t-shirt. He raised her shirt and guided it over her head, revealing a modest red bikini top. He dropped the shirt to the floor. His hands released the snaps at her waist and the overalls fell to her ankles. Mesmerized, she stepped slowly out of them, shoving them to the side. He reached behind her head and untied the bandana knot to release the soft red curls that fell past her shoulders.

Eddie stared. "A minute ago you looked like a maintenance worker, dressed to paint the harbor. Now, you look sexy. I don't understand why you don't clean the boat dressed like this. Some sun wouldn't hurt you. Let me guess—you're afraid you wouldn't be taken seriously by the crew."

She put her hands on her hips. "You mean walk around half-naked? Being taken seriously isn't even—"

"Not now." He put one hand over her mouth and the other behind her back, pulling her close.

Her body tightened and she thought about letting go and feeling the excitement she had experienced and then denied the other night. She wished she could be more like Gina and Amy and enjoy casual sex, especially here in summer Newport, where it seemed to be part of the landscape. But before this went any further, she was determined to know where she stood. She pulled his hand from her lips.

"Are we leaving this lighthouse as more than friends?"

"Probably not. We can leave here as friends, or we can leave here as friends who took advantage of an empty lighthouse."

"I don't know," Margo bit her lip, but she *did* know. She knew she didn't want sex with Eddie to be casual. In fact, she understood it *couldn't* be.

"I know you," he predicted. "You're already trying to calculate what this will mean to us when we get back to school. I don't want to think that far ahead. Hell, I'm still trying to get over how you look in that bikini."

"What if we go downstairs for a dip? I bet the water's nice and warm." She tried to turn toward the door.

"I'm taking a dip, but it's not in the water."

He kissed her. His mouth felt hard. The weight of anxiety she felt began to subside as he embraced her, overwhelmed by just plain wanting him. He lifted her by the waist, and she reflexively wrapped her legs around him. He carried her to the bed and threw her down, then straddled her, resting on his knees. Bending over, he covered the outline of her bathing suit with wet kisses, using his hands to fumble a condom out of his pocket and unzip his jeans.

He was all impatience after that, pulling off her bikini bottoms and sliding between her legs. Then, it was all ecstasy and the synchronized movement of their bodies. At the moment she cried out in release, she heard a man's voice echo her as if from a distance. It was the same sound she had heard the first night they were together in Eddie's dorm room.

"Did you hear that?" she asked Eddie, but he only grunted and sighed.

"Don't hear a damn thing."

7

September 1977

IKE LAST YEAR, MARGO was the last to arrive, so she got relegated to the top bunk. Unpacking plastic bags filled with sweaters, a hot pot, shampoo in half pint bottles, and hot chocolate mix, she stored them in her dresser drawer and the little space left in the shared closet. She recognized Gina's theatre books on the single bed and Amy's tattered overalls strewn across the bottom bunk.

As she stuffed her socks in the bottom drawer, she felt good to be back in the familiar setting. The girls had won the first lottery pick of dorm selections, and to Margo's delight, had chosen room 405 Francis again, despite Gina's desire to try new digs.

She glanced out the large sliding windows overlooking the quad and spied some of Eddie's teammates crossing the path. A few weeks ago, Margo had bid Eddie farewell on that unforeseen afternoon at the Newport lighthouse. If she was being totally honest with herself, she'd admit the ache for him wouldn't go away. But back here at school, he was a hot commodity with many girls. She contemplated tutoring him, and imagined one long session at the library might lead to a night of passion. But what would be next? He'd never commit to her and would always be looking for his next conquest.

She had made up her mind to treat him like a science experiment she could easily execute, then forget. She envisioned pouring last year's and the summer's memories into a beaker, along with a potion to vaporize her memories and her current feelings.

After Margo finished unpacking, she noticed a note taped to the mirror above their little vanity. It read, "Meet us in the parking lot at noon, luv, your roomies." She realized she only had a few minutes, and hurried to hurl her heavy coat and outer garments into the chest at the foot of the bunk bed. Then she slid the window open, caught Gina and Amy's attention, and motioned she was on her way down.

* * *

Across campus, Eddie dribbled the ball out of the gym and made his way west, across the courtyard and onto the walkway toward Francis Hall. Halfway there, he stopped and pulled out a folded piece of paper from his pocket with his free hand. Tucking the basketball under his arm, he read the report again. His eyes moved to the box on the right hand side of the paper. Under classification, the word *dyslexic* was circled. Margo had been right. Now he understood all the years in school why his classmates thought he was stupid: He read things backwards. He folded the paper and slipped it back into his pocket.

Eddie's mind was preoccupied with a number of other concerns. One was how to get through the new semester without flunking any classes. Another was shouldering the responsibility that came with his recent appointment to Team Captain. Although enthusiastic about the chance to lead his team to a possible championship, he knew from their performance in recent practices that the team had a long way to go to be playoff caliber. He had confided in his father that he secretly hoped he would get passed over as Captain. That disclosure left Eddie with a black eye and a lecture about shirking responsibility. He gingerly rubbed his still slightly swollen right eye.

Eddie expected another black eye when his father found out about his son's learning disability. To Eddie's relief, his father's reaction was the opposite of what he'd anticipated. He seemed almost remorseful and promised to be supportive. Eddie felt he owed this to Margo, because her tenacity had brought about his diagnosis. That train of thought led to the third and most important problem: *what to do about Margo*. Satisfied that he'd conquered her sexually once and for all, he felt sure there'd be no more "I don't know." No more reluctance.

Even though Margo's idea of wild behavior was mixing up hypotheses about cross-pollination, he couldn't erase the memory of her standing before him in that red bikini. And though her sexual performance hadn't disappointed him, it hadn't blown him away either. He left that job to Amy. It made him dizzy just remembering how wild she'd been with him on the bow of the *Thomas Tew* that night in Newport.

He shook off thoughts of Amy. He'd checked with Professor Turner this morning and Margo had still not reinstated her tutoring assignment. He'd been sure that, after their time together—and especially with the dyslexia thing—she'd want to pick up where they'd left off. Now it looked like he'd have to persuade her to change her mind.

Eddie reached Francis Hall and trotted up the front steps to the house monitor's desk in the lobby.

"Can you buzz room 405 and tell Margo that Eddie's waiting downstairs to meet her?"

* * *

Margo was on the third step from the bottom of the staircase when she heard his voice. She almost turned around to go back upstairs, but knew Gina and Amy were expecting her in the parking lot. Margo, aware she'd have to see him sooner or later, had nevertheless hoped to delay the reckoning as long as possible. Why today? She took a deep breath, exhaled, and continued down the stairs.

"Oh, hey, there you are," Eddie greeted her. "I was hoping you'd be wearing that red bikini."

"We're not in Newport anymore," Margo rebuffed him. "I'm assuming you know I'm not tutoring you this semester."

"I thought we were going to pick up where we left off over the summer. I got serious. Can't we just go back to the way it was?"

"I'm just too busy with extra lab work." Margo avoided his stare and tried to flatten the creases in her gingham shorts.

"You're lying," Eddie accused.

"Why would I lie?"

"Tell me the real reason you don't want to tutor me."

"You're better off with a tutor who specializes in learning disabilities. I have to go," Margo took a step forward.

Eddie blocked her from the front entrance. "I can change

your mind. Meet me in the student lounge one night this week?"
Eddie pleaded, but Margo sidestepped around him and scurried
out the front door.

* * *

Gina's red Mustang was a masterpiece of elegance and engi-
neering: red leather seats, convertible top, stick shift, V8 power.

"Nice wheels," Margo whistled as she hopped in the back seat
behind Amy.

Gina remembered the morning her consolation prize had
arrived the week after she returned home from the Newport
Jazz Fest, still stung by the afterimage of Carlos with String
Bikini Babe.

Gina had confronted her parents about her desire to transfer
from CHP to Rhode Island Tech school. She'd completed the
RIT paperwork on the sly and sat patiently at the dining room
table one night, while her parents paced the room and spoke in
hushed Italian.

When they finally turned to her, Gina's dad said, "Your
brother, Salvatore, told us that queer painter you chased around
in high school is an assistant Art teacher this year at RIT. Is this
what this transfer nonsense is all about?"

Carlos' new job was news to Gina, but it gave her all the
more reason to transfer: she couldn't resist the thought of being
closer to Carlos. Her parents said nothing more, but told her to
go to bed and they would sleep on it.

They'd done more than sleep on it. For three days they
deliberated. The following Monday, Gina awakened to the sight
of her beaming parents standing over her bed, while her father
dangled a gold key chain over her. She knew then art school was

out of the question. Instead of a transfer, she'd go back to her vanilla life at CHP, but with new wheels to soften the blow. If only she could switch to RIT, her life would be so much better. Still, she was grateful for the gift and thanked them profusely for giving her second prize.

Still in the Francis Hall parking lot, Gina revved the engine and rolled the windows down. She tried to focus on the car's sleek shine while she primped her thick black hair in the rear-view mirror.

"Let's truck over to the East side," she suggested as she maneuvered out of the busy parking lot.

"Let me guess—RIT?" Margo asked.

"Yes, but this time, the visit will be more exciting," Gina promised.

"Why, because we're cruising in style?" Amy inquired.

"Uh-huh, and because Carlos is a teacher's aid there."

"Oh no! This could be dangerous," Amy laughed.

"While we're on the subject of Carlos," Gina prodded, pulling onto Yarmouth Street, "let's talk about the Blind Date Ball. It's the first Friday in October, so we don't have much time. I know we're supposed to surprise each other with dates, but the three of us should have some say in who we'll go with. Don't you agree?"

"Let me guess." Margo leaned forward so that her arms rested on the top of the front seat. "Are Amy and I asking Carlos for you?"

"I want to go with Eddie Sullivan," Amy interrupted, "but there will probably be a line around the corner, so we better ask him today."

Gina watched in the rear view mirror as Margo sank back into her seat. She could just kick Amy sometimes.

"I'm not sure I even want to go," Margo stated dully.

Amy turned to Margo. "What are you talking about? You have to go. Gina and I can find someone perfect for you, right Gina?"

Damn Amy, anyway, Gina thought. Margo's face in the rear view mirror wore a blank expression. "Maybe Margo has someone in mind," Gina suggested.

Margo gazed stoically out the window.

"Really? " Amy remarked, turning around to stare at Margo.

"Or maybe this year I'll concentrate on studying," Margo declared. "It's pathetic how boy crazy some girls are."

"Suit yourself," Amy responded, turning back around. "Hey, can you pull over? I need to grab a pack of gum from the deli." Gina and Margo exchanged a quick look as Gina maneuvered the car into the crowded parking lot.

Once Amy had disappeared into the store, Gina turned to Margo in the backseat. "I know there's something going on between you and Eddie," Gina accused. "You can't hide that stuff from me. I see the way you look at him. I noticed the way you pined for him last semester. Did something happen over the summer?"

Margo waved her hand dismissively. "We had a brief … thing. Just once, when I got caught up in that hot Newport summer air. " She chuckled, but her laughter sounded thin and forced.

"Yeah, talk about hot air…"

"You know how the sea breezes can cloud a girl's brain and make her do things she wouldn't normally do," Margo added.

"Uh-huh." Gina glanced back at the store, where Amy flirted with the tall cashier at the register, batting her false eyelashes and flipping her long hair around. "All right, then. Eddie will go with Amy and I'll ask that nerdy lab partner of yours. Ted, right?"

"God," Margo sighed. "The whole thing is so painfully old-fashioned. I really don't want to go. What about you? Do you want me to ask Carlos?"

"I think he's dating that bottle-blonde bimbo from the boat. She's his nude model now." Gina's throat tightened as tears threatened. She fought them back, thankful for her sunglasses.

"Oh, please," Margo coaxed. "You know if you say the word, Carlos will come running back to you. Talk about the way I look at Eddie— Do you see how Carlos stares at you? The guy is in love."

Amy got back in the car and they continued to cruise the east side of Providence. Once they were within a few blocks of RIT, Gina scanned the streets for a parking space. She got lucky; a station wagon pulled out of a slot just across the street from the main buildings and Gina pulled easily into the vacant spot.

The girls piled out of the car and crossed the street. It was the first day of the faculty moving-in process, so several teachers milled around the lobby of the Fine Arts building. Among the many canvasses hanging on the wall, one immediately caught Gina's eye: a larger-than-life nude blonde. Gina recognized the model with no trouble—she was the blonde who'd been with Carlos on the boat at the Newport Jazz Festival.

"What do you think?" Gina turned to the other girls and blanched as she saw Carlos striding toward them. "Well,"she said tightly, "speak of the devil…"

Carlos nodded to Amy and Margo, then moved to Gina's side. He glanced from her to the painting and back, then murmured so softly only she could hear, "I would rather have painted you."

"There' s still time," Gina retorted, then damned all and continued: "Why didn't you tell me you were working here?

You know I've been dying to transfer to RIT. We could've been together."

He shook his head, his smile more of a grimace. "It was you, not me, who didn't want to be tied down. You have your pick of the litter with guys your age over at that preppy high school. What's the use of trying again?"

She turned to look up into his face. God, but she loved it. She had memorized its every detail. "Maybe we could? I don't know—maybe if we take it slow."

"Maybe," Carlos considered, after a moment. He seemed unable to break away from Gina's intent gaze.

Maybe Margo was right, Gina thought. Maybe—

Margo interrupted, "Gina, why don't you wait in the car with Amy? I want to talk to Carlos for a minute."

Gina glanced at Margo and smiled. Her best friend was going to help her fix this. She just knew it.

Amy looped her arm through Gina's and led her back out to the parking lot.

* * *

"What's this about?" Carlos asked his brow furrowed. "Advice for the lovelorn?"

Margo laughed. "Nothing like that. Just an invitation to the Blind Date Ball. You know, the one where friends fix up other friends with the perfect date."

He shoved his hands into his jacket pockets. "Ah, yes. That old ritual. And you're asking me for Gina?"

Margo nodded. "Please," she pleaded solemnly. "You two are like ... fated or something."

He chuckled. "Or something ... but, yes. Okay. I'll do it."

97

"Great," Margo exclaimed, "It's the first weekend in October. We're all meeting on the lawn, then walking over to Alumni Hall. I'll call you with the details."

Margo hurried away to rejoin her friends.

Behind her, she heard Carlos murmur, "God help me."

8

O N THE FIRST FRIDAY night of October, Margo, Gina, and Amy loitered in the quad in front of Francis Hall, waiting with the rest of the dorm residents for their dates for the blind date ball to show. A flock of boys, all neatly dressed in sport shirts and slacks, approached them.

Margo picked Ted out of the pack and waved. His eyes lit up when he saw her, and she was suddenly thankful she had taken the time to dress with care in a v-neck, check pattern mini-dress, with low-heeled loafers. Her smile froze on her face when she caught sight of Eddie arriving from the far side of the quad. He sported a red shirt with an alligator on the breast under a navy blazer with three gold buttons on each sleeve, and tan khakis. His stare pierced Margo as he ambled toward the three girls. She caught her breath.

Eddie held her gaze until he was practically face-to-face with Amy, and only then looked away from Margo. Amy, dressed to impress in white bell bottoms, a crocheted waistcoat, and a tight, scoop-neck sweater, clearly made an impact on Eddie; his gaze dropped to her cleavage. Margo's sudden exhilaration dropped with it.

Gina squeezed her elbow and whispered, "I know, Eddie

looks foxy. But try to have a good time with Ted. He's thrilled to be your date."

"Thanks. I know I'll have a nice time," Margo assured her, and turned her attention to Ted, flashing him a big smile.

Anya stood in the middle of the group of forty or so students. "Girls, before we go, I'm gonna put on my RA hat for a moment, okay? I don't want any of you getting sick, so if you want to run back upstairs and grab your umbrellas, hats, gloves, whatever, it's supposed to hail later. It's already pretty cold." As if to make the point, she exhaled a banner of steam.

"I can run upstairs and throw our stuff into a tote bag," Gina told Margo. "Carlos isn't here yet, anyway."

"Good idea," Margo agreed. "My winter stuff is in the chest at the foot of the bunk. Can you grab my slicker, brown hat, and red mittens?"

"Sure. I'll meet you at Alumni Hall. Don't hit the dance floor without me."

"Where *is* Carlos?" Margo asked.

"I guess he's meeting me at the dance. He has to stay late on Fridays and Saturdays to grade projects." Gina took off at a trot back toward the dorm.

Margo started to turn to Ted, but Eddie stepped between them and pulled Margo aside. Ted forgot to be the adoring fan and glared at the other boy.

"Can you excuse me a moment?" Margo murmured, then let Eddie draw her away a few paces.

She knew what was coming; Professor Turner had relayed to her that Eddie was reluctant to work with a new tutor. Margo had avoided his phone calls for weeks.

"I need to talk to you," Eddie demanded.

"We're talking now."

"I mean seriously. Soon. Tonight, if we can."

"I thought we already covered tutoring."

"This isn't about tutoring," Eddie muttered, moving closer.

Margo backed away. "I gotta go. Maybe I'll see you on the dance floor." She fled back to Ted, and together they joined the student group headed to the upper campus.

Inside Alumni Hall, two hours into the dance, Margo swayed at one corner of the dance floor to the beat of the Kink's song, *Lola*. The temperature in the large room rose uncomfortably from the heat of many bodies, and she gratefully accepted the glass of ginger ale Ted offered. Momentarily closing her eyes, she rested the cool glass against her sweaty forehead. She opened her eyes again to view students pulsating on the crowded dance floor. Then her gaze turned to Eddie and Amy, slow dancing, their arms wrapped around each other's necks.

"Wanna dance?" Ted asked.

"Maybe later," Margo replied.

"I'm excited for later," Ted smiled, giving her a significant 'look.'

"Are you talking about the late night party at the Rugby House?"

"I'll go anywhere you want, but Jason, my biology partner, kyped the lab keys, so the science group is meeting there at midnight after this ends."

"To do what?"

"Party. We packed a cooler of beers. Hid it in the custodian's closet."

Margo shrugged. "We could go the rugby party or the lab party. I don't care."

Ted's fingers clumsily caressed the back of her neck. "Wanna swig?" he offered, pulling a flask from his khaki pocket with his free hand.

Margo looked out at the dance floor at Amy snuggling into Eddie's neck and whispering into his ear.

"Sure," she acquiesced, "I'll take some of whatever you're serving." She held out her glass of ginger ale and watched Teddy pour a clear liquid into her drink. She took a gulp, then another, and wished she'd eaten something more substantial than an apple for dinner.

Gina bounced up to Margo and Ted on the arm of a brawny guy Margo recognized from around campus. He caught sight of Ted's flask and gave him a thumbs-up.

"Let me get you a drink, gorgeous," he told Gina. "Gimme something to sustain me on the way." He tried to kiss her on the lips but missed when she moved her head away.

"Drink first," she ordered, shoving him lightly.

"Sure. The real stuff's hidden in the cooler out back." He made a wobbly turn and disappeared into the crowd.

* * *

"Anybody seen my date yet?" Gina inquired.

"Looks like you're doing fine without him," Margo noted wryly.

But she wasn't doing fine. She seldom did fine without Carlos. Where was he? Gina double-checked her watch and decided he must be stuck at school.

"Maybe I'll go wait for him outside. It's too hot in here, anyway."

She slipped out of Alumni Hall, shivering in her light coat as she hurried north to the Francis dormitory parking lot where she'd left her Mustang. The rain had turned to a mix of sleet and hail. The parking lot and surrounding area remained practically empty.

Thoroughly soaked by the time she reached the car, Gina wasted no time starting the engine and blasting the heater at full power. She pulled out of the parking lot and snaked southward through the campus, windshield wipers working overtime to clear the sleet and hail. Finally the heater kicked in; by the time she exited campus and turned toward the main gate, she had begun to thaw out.

She drove to the east side, bypassed the main RIT entrance and went around to the faculty apartments, located a short city block from the academic halls. She circled the block twice before finding a parking spot on the busy street. Braving the elements again, she climbed the steps to the entrance, grateful for the awning that sheltered her somewhat from the increasingly bad weather.

She repeatedly buzzed Carlos's apartment, to no avail. Unwilling to admit defeat, she rang a couple of bells until someone buzzed her in. Finding his apartment unlocked, she opened the door and entered his tiny white tiled vestibule. She hesitated for a moment, unsure of her next step.

Why in the world would he stand her up? She stomped into the living room, where a small oak desk stood against the wall, its surface covered with a messy pile of papers. A calendar rested on top.

Gina moved to the desk and turned the calendar to read it. An entry was noted on tonight's date in Carlos's neat cursive: "Poetry reading." She flipped to the Saturday page. "Blind Date Ball" stood out in bold red marker, underlined twice.

He thinks the dance is tomorrow night. Gina pulled a pen from her purse and wrote on the calendar's Friday page, "The Blind Date Ball was tonight, not tomorrow. When you get back from poetry, meet me at 2:00 AM outside in the Francis quad. I'll be waiting for you."

Then she slipped out of the apartment.

* * *

Margo's equilibrium slipped as her body started to feel the effects of the alcohol. Ted suggested they get some fresh air. He led her through the crowd toward the front door, then paused.

"Let me fill up our glasses at the bar and spike them before we go outside. Wait here."

Margo closed her eyes and leaned back against the wall.

"How's your date going?"

Margo opened her eyes. It was Eddie, of course, standing so close to her she could almost feel the heat radiating off his body.

"Sneaking up on me again?" she asked.

He studied her for a moment, then leaned in and kissed her.

"Who gave you permission to kiss me?" she demanded when her lips were free again.

"Come to the keg party with me."

"Ted and I have other plans."

"I need to talk to you," Eddie entreated. He put one hand on the wall behind her. "Why don't we just sneak outside for ten minutes. Just ten minutes. Nobody will miss us."

Margo felt something inside of her sink, but kept her face impassive. "Well, all right. I suppose we can chat for a few minutes outside on the front steps. As long as Ted's still at the bar."

But Ted had already come back. "Last call, Sullivan. You better drink up."

Eddie straightened and turned toward Ted. "Maybe I'll see you guys at the rugby party. I'm heading over there now. "

Ted looked at Margo. "So what do you think, lab or Rugby House?

"Rugby," Margo decided.

* * *

The dance ended at midnight, but Eddie and Amy hung back a little, letting the pack of exiting students get a little distance ahead. Hail pellets continued to pound down, as the temperature dipped into the low forties. Amy pulled out the slicker she'd stashed in her macramé bag and tugged it over her head while Eddie struggled to open the folding umbrella he'd carried in his jacket pocket. Together, they ventured out into the inhospitable night, both trying to shelter under Eddie's small umbrella.

They arrived at the rugby party on the heels of the slower students from the dance. Amy shrugged off her cold weather gear and made a beeline for a couch, while Eddie lent a hand to tapping the kegs of beer. He returned to Amy after a few minutes with a glass in each hand.

"Give me your slicker and I'll toss our stuff into one of the bedrooms," Eddie suggested, handing her a beer. "I may smoke a joint in the basement with some of the guys, so I'll be back in a bit."

Amy didn't look happy about that plan, but she just shrugged and handed Eddie her rain gear. He quickly made his way through the crowded living room of the old mansion to one of the guest bedrooms where he threw the rainwear on the cluttered bed, which was serving as a makeshift closet.

Eddie followed the smell of marijuana to the house's large

kitchen. There a ring of students, passed a joint from hand to hand. Eddie started for the circle, then spotted Margo and Ted in a darkened corner of the room. Looked like all they were doing was talking. Ted was a moron.

He hesitated. He hadn't been able to keep his eyes off Margo the entire night. All he'd wanted to do the whole time was drag her away from the other guy and take her home. Maybe Eddie should just poke Ted, the lab nerd, in the nose.

Eddie had begun to move toward them when he felt a soft hand on his arm and heard Amy's throaty voice in his ear: "Let's go upstairs."

Brain short-circuited, Eddie let Amy steer him past Ted and Margo to the back door, where a servants' staircase led to the upper floors. The light was off. Amy took Eddie's hand and guided him into the darkened stairwell. He thought about the last time he'd been with Amy and felt heat sweep through his groin.

"Is there something upstairs that you want to show me?" he asked, suddenly breathless.

"Keep climbing." Amy coaxed, backing up the stairs one at a time, holding both of his hands. At the midway point, she stopped, let go of his hands, and grabbed the waist of his pants to pull him closer. His eyes were level with her breasts.

He took a quick breath and got an instant hard on. He groaned inwardly. The night wasn't going according to plan. He would rather be with Margo who was just down there, in the kitchen. Just a few feet away. He'd planned to tell her he wanted to move forward with her and for things to return to the way they had been before he'd cheated on that stupid test. But the feel of Amy's hands tugging at his pants as she pulled him farther up the stairwell derailed all thoughts.

He climbed another step, tried to collect himself. "Hey, let's-let's go down and smoke a joint first." Eddie took a deep breath. "Smell that, baby? Let's get mellow."

"There's plenty of time to get mellow," Amy whispered seductively. "I have a little smoking of my own to do."

She'd reached the second floor landing and started to unfasten his pants. He closed his eyes. He did still want to talk to Margo, but his eagerness to reunite with her was lost in the heat he felt as Amy's hands made their way down to his zipper. He was losing focus. When she dropped to her knees on the top step and lifted his shirt to plant a kiss on his navel, he lost it altogether. He dropped his pants. Amy's expert hands moved south and there was no turning back.

He would talk to Margo tomorrow.

* * *

It was 1:00 AM. Margo woke from a sound sleep, vaguely aware that something was not quite right. She climbed down from the top bunk and peered around to orient herself. Light from the hallway spilled into the girls' room. Margo used it to navigate to Gina's bed and shook her roommate awake.

"Gina, maybe I'm crazy, but I think I smell smoke. Do you smell it, too?"

"No ... well, maybe." She bolted upright. "Yeah, I do smell smoke! Wonder where it's coming from?"

"I don't know." Margo felt her way to the light switch and flipped it on. "I'm going to check the hallway."

Margo grabbed her blue cotton bathrobe from the bed post and secured it with a tight knot, as she scanned the bottom bunk. Empty. "Amy must be bunking somewhere else," she surmised.

With Eddie, she didn't say.

"Forget about that for now," Gina advised and swung her legs over the side of her bed. "I'm glad you woke me up. I'm supposed to meet Carlos outside in an hour. I tried to stay up, but I must have dozed off."

Margo stared at Amy's bed and wondered why she had been fooled by Eddie. All that sober talk about wanting to discuss something more than tutoring. If what he had to say was so important, why didn't he find her at the rugby party later? She had caught him staring at her in the kitchen. For a couple of seconds, she felt an electric charge between them as he approached her. But then Ted had run interference and when she'd looked again, Eddie had disappeared. Now, after a sloppy goodnight kiss from Ted and a few hours of sleep, her mind still swirled with thoughts of Eddie.

She ventured into the hall and looked left and right. To her left, tendrils of smoke crept from beneath the closed bathroom door. Fear tightened her throat. She hurried to the bathroom door, placed a hand against the wood, and recoiled from the heat. Turning back, truly scared now, she ran to her room to find Gina rummaging for something to wear.

"I think there's a fire in the bathroom," Margo cried out. "Smoke is seeping out into the hallway. We'd better start knocking on doors to wake everybody up!"

Wasting no time, the girls burst into the hallway, already half-filled with smoke. They pounded desperately on the other bedroom doors yelling, "Fire!"

Sleepy students emerged from their rooms as the smoke thickened and darkened. Margo took charge. "Everybody to the front staircase and make your way down. Wake everybody on the lower floors. I'll go to the corner rooms and get the rest of the girls up here."

Gina grabbed Margo's arm. "Don't leave me! You can't pass the bathroom alone—that's where the smoke is coming from. What if it gets worse?"

"Fine, let's go."

Margo headed resolutely away from the safety of the staircase with Gina tagging behind. They hurried past the bathroom—the door was now in flames. Margo fought panic as she pounded on the door of the four bed suite shared by the Swedish exchange students. The girls tumbled out into the hall, eyes wide with fear as smoke eddied around them.

Margo directed Gina to the three-bed suite across the hall, while she banged on the RA's door.

Anya appeared fully dressed, and hugged Margo. "I'm already up. Are the eight of us from this corner all here?"

Margo saw the four cheerleaders who bunked in room 411 standing next to Gina. She took a head count. "All here."

A strange ripping sound filled the air and sparks sprayed out into the back hall from the main corridor. One of the cheerleaders screamed. Margo dashed back to the intersection of the two hallways and witnessed the cause of the terrified girls' screams: the flames vaulted from the bathroom door to the ceiling, which now rained down chunks of burning plaster into the corridor. Sheets of blazing wallpaper peeled from the walls and fell to the floor. The carpet runner caught fire.

They were cut off from the staircase and safety.

Margo pointed up the transverse hallway toward the front of the house. "We can't get past the bathroom, so let's go back into the four-bed suite. It's the farthest from the flames."

She herded the nine other girls into the room and closed the door behind them.

Inside, the air wasn't as smoky, but it was only a matter of time before the smoke and flames made their way here. The girls opened the window and took turns leaning out to breathe fresh air.

* * *

Amy lay naked on her stomach next to Eddie on the bed of his solitary dorm room. He rolled onto his side and stroked her back as if she were a pet cat. As if catching his thought, she purred.

Eddie chuckled and put his lips to her ear. "Roll over."

"Back for round two?" Amy asked.

"Round three if you count the stairwell."

"Have it your way," she turned over.

Eddie leaned over and kissed her neck.

She giggled. "Tickles," she protested.

"Shut up," he murmured. "There'll be hell to pay if the house 'dad' finds out you're here." And then his own dad would probably beat the crap out of him.

A hard bang on the door made them both jump. Eddie turned, panicking. But the person who came through the door into the darkened room was his next-door neighbor, Chuck.

"What the fuck, man?" Eddie yelled and rolled over while Amy scrambled to pull the sheet up over her naked body.

Chuck stood awkwardly in the doorway, looking scared. "Francis Hall is on fire."

* * *

Even though the girls took turns breathing by the window, smoke seeped into the room and the temperature grew hotter and hotter. Margo and Gina huddled side by side at the window trying to suck in fresh air from outside. They'd pushed out the screen so they could take turns leaning out, like Gina.

"I'm getting dizzy," Gina sobbed.

"You're leaning too far out of the window! Get back in!"

Margo pulled Gina into the room and turned to the others. They huddled as close to the window as they could, crying. Margo stood firm.

"Put something over your noses to filter the smoke. The firemen will be here soon; we have to stay calm. Anya, grab something to shove under the door so no more smoke can get in."

Anya and another girl stripped one of the beds and stuffed the blankets under the door sill.

By now, the heat had begun to overwhelm them. Margo felt as though she were standing in front of a pizza oven. As more smoke crept into the room, the others started to wail, calling out for their mothers. Margo cupped her face with both hands and fought hysteria.

"Everyone stay calm. Breathe shallow and keep your noses and mouths covered."

Coughing, the girls obeyed, some pulling their shirts up over their noses, almost burying their heads in their clothes.

"It's too hot!" Gina cried in a shrill voice. "Where the fuck are the firemen? I need more air." Yanking Margo aside, Gina turned back to the window and leaned out. "What's taking so long?"

Margo brushed Gina's tears away with the sleeve of her bathrobe and noticed her own hands shaking uncontrollably. She leaned out the window alongside Gina, peering into the large parking lot four stories below. She could see students under the dim parking lot lights but nothing else. Then, she thought she heard sirens.

"They're here!" Margo shouted. "The firemen are on their way! We'll be all right."

Margo's sense of time had warped since they'd entered the room, but she knew it had been long enough to make breathing a challenge. Her lungs labored. She'd had enough biology to know her brain wasn't getting enough oxygen. Tears blurred her eyesight, the scene below swam in front of her, and the sound of the fire alarms and sirens became muffled.

* * *

Eddie frantically threw on sweats and a t-shirt, telling Amy, "Stay put. I'm going with Chuck and the others."

"But, Margo and Gina—"

Margo.

Eddie ignored Amy and raced out the door and down the hall. Outside, he joined with the rest of the boys from the lower campus dorms. He glanced across the campus at the swarm of students running north at full speed. He ran flat out, passing most of them, flying past the baseball and rugby fields. Through the dark air and sleet still pounding the ground, he reached the lane that divided upper and lower campus. Fire trucks lined up at the upper campus entrance, their sirens blaring. Several police cars and ambulances followed close behind. But students' parked cars filled the lot, making it difficult for the fire trucks to get near the burning building.

Groups of students gathered along the street, some boys in little more than their underwear, others in sweats, only a few fully dressed. Firemen stood next to the first fire truck that made it into the lot, blocked by a row of cars from getting the access necessary to reach the building with their hoses and ladders.

Eddie approached one of the firemen and yelled over the sirens, "How are you gonna get the trucks to Francis?"

"We have to get the cars out of the way," the fireman shouted back. "How do you feel about pushing cars to the side to free a path?"

Eddie turned the boys around him and gestured at the row of parked cars. "We're going to have to push the cars closest to Francis out of the way to clear a path for the fire trucks."

They suited action to word, leading his squad of students to the first car in the fire truck's path—a dark green Pinto. He tried the doors first, but it was locked. He called four other students to him around the car, shouting instructions: "When I count to three, push the car back out of the space, okay? One, two, *three*."

Eddie pushed the car with all of his might; it resisted, then groaned and began to roll backward toward the opposite side of the row.

"All the way out! All the way!" Eddie cried, pushing harder.

Another group of boys had surrounded the car in the next space over, and found it unlocked. One of the boys got in and flipped off the parking brake. His companions rolled the car away from the curb.

Too damn slow, Eddie thought, launching himself at the next available car. Until now, he thought he had all the time in the world to make it right with Margo. It hadn't been a matter of him not wanting to give up his freedom in exchange for a serious commitment to her. He figured she sensed his confusion and that was why she had been avoiding him. There were questions that needed answers, problems that needed solving. Before this moment, there had been time. Now, it seemed there might be none.

After twenty minutes, Eddie and his cohort had moved the entire row of cars enough to allow a train of fire trucks and police cars to pull closer to Francis Hall. Eddie ran to join hundreds of students congregated outside the dorm. He looked for girls he recognized as Francis Hall residents; some stood huddled beneath a spreading oak tree, crying, some were already being helped toward an ambulance. He scanned the girls for Margo and Gina. His gut told him he wouldn't see them here, and he looked up at the corner window of the fourth floor. Two girls were silhouetted against a lurid red light. Were they Margo and Gina? He shuddered to think what they must be going through, trapped between hungry flames and a forty foot drop to concrete. He knew Margo. She wouldn't leave unless she knew everyone had been safely evacuated, and he suspected Gina would be too scared to leave her side.

Hearing the whine and growl of a motor, Eddie turned to watch the firemen begin the process of extending a telescoping ladder from the nearest truck. A firefighter already clinging to the lowest segment waited for the upper segment of the ladder to deploy.

Eddie turned back to the dorm and cupped his hands around his mouth. "Don't do anything stupid!" he shouted, desperation making his voice crack. "They're coming for you."

He had no idea if they could hear him—probably not—but he had to try. He told himself that they'd soon be climbing down to safety. That soon he would see Margo and hold her in his arms. She'd be okay. He told himself that, then realized that the firetruck's ladder still couldn't reach all the way to the window. The girls would have to leap…

The thought made him queasy. He started toward where the fireman working the ladder conferred with the Chief of Police. Just as he reached them, he heard the fireman say, "I don't think the girls can see the ladder and I'm not sure they can all make that jump; it's got to be about four feet. This isn't good."

Eddie doubled over and vomited on the wet parking lot.

* * *

"I can't take it!" Gina cried. "My whole body is burning up. And the smell, it's so horrible."

"Hold onto me." Margo turned around to seek the others in the dark room, but the smoke obscured her vision. She could barely see Gina. She could only feel Gina's hands clamped onto her arm, her nails digging in, clawing deeper and deeper into her skin, making Margo feel as if they'd cut her to the bone.

Margo's breath came in short, shallow gasps, as if each might be her last. And the heat—the heat was too much to bear. Stripping off her bathrobe hadn't helped. She tried to stay focused by recounting the scientific facts about smoke inhalation. How much time did they have? How much more could her lungs tolerate? None of that mattered right now. She wanted her mother.

A high-pitched whining sound erupted behind her. She squinted through the haze in the dorm room and there it was: the wooden door was ablaze, flames licking upward, devouring the varnished wood.

PART II

"WHOM THE GODS LOVE DIE YOUNG."

— PLAUTUS

9

That Same Night—October 13, 1977

T HE ACRID, STINGING SMOKE carried a stew of scents—burning fabric, wood, and plaster—charred meat. Margo didn't want to think about that. The unbearable heat seared the tears from her eyes, making deserts of her cheeks.

She sagged toward the window, felt the frame against her shoulder, then cooler air caressed her face. A voice, insistent and frantic, struggled to cut through the sounds of fire and fear and the groaning, dying building.

With the suddenness of a door slamming shut, the roar of the fire and the shouts of their rescuers muted, seeming to come to her through wads of cotton.

God, it was so hard to breathe …

… and then it wasn't, and she thought she smelled her mother's fresh baked apple pie.

Why would death smell like apple pie?

Something struck her, and she felt the rush of cool air, as if she were floating. Thank God, it was over. It was over and her lungs no longer burned.

She heard nothing now; saw nothing. Her eyes were closed. She opened them.

It's just as I imagined it would be, Margo thought as she took in the view. She was no longer in the dorm. She didn't know where she was, but a stunning 360-degree view of a garden carpeted in soft, green grass stretched in front of her. Sloping paths and streams that sparkled like liquid crystal and cascaded into pools of limpid blue-green threaded through the landscape. The walkways seemed to all lead to rose gardens. Distant buildings resembled old-world universities—Cambridge, maybe, or Oxford.

Margo felt … How did she feel? Stunned. Disoriented. But did she feel *dead*?

Only hours ago, she'd been hanging out at a campus party, anxiously waiting for Eddie to make his move. Only he hadn't. He'd wanted to, though, Margo had felt it—had been certain of it. He had been close to confiding in her, to making things right between them. Tonight, at the dance, for the first time since their last day together at the lighthouse in Newport, Eddie's motives seemed genuine.

She smiled as she remembered his urgently whispered, "I need to talk to you."

Wherever she was, she felt elated … safe. She bounced lightly on her bare feet, then looked down to see what sort of grass was so springy. Perfect grass, she decided, is that springy. It was like something you'd find on a golf course, its texture a cross between velvet and fleece. The ground sloped away from her into a shallow glen from which a silvery mist rose to slink along the streams and curl up through the trees.

Green fleece underfoot, she struck off for the mouth of the closest path. The mist thickened around her as she dipped into the glen and navigated the stream bed. This proved to be no more difficult than walking across a tiny half-moon bridge like the ones she'd seen in Japanese tea gardens and home and garden magazines.

When she emerged from the mist, she discovered a man standing at the trail head beneath a sign that read, *Halfway*. She first noticed his hair, which was blond, wavy, shoulder length, and far too pretty to be wasted on a guy. His blue eyes seemed to be laughing at her, and the white shirt and dark blue pants he wore—which were close-fitting and capri length—showed a well-muscled body to advantage. He wasn't buff like a body-builder, but looked as if he came by his muscles honestly.

She might have taken him for a college student if it weren't for the oddly old-world clothing and the large antique cross hanging on a thick golden chain about his neck. Staring at the cross, she knew she had seen him before, but couldn't connect with the knowledge.

"So, you're the group leader from Christopher Hayes Prep," he remarked.

"I'm not a group leader … what are you talking about?" Margo asked.

His eyes glinted with humor. "I don't make the rules around here, darling girl, I just make certain everyone follows them."

Just as cocky as Eddie, she thought, meeting his gaze. She considered being saucy right back, but that tone never really worked for her. Instead, she composed herself and stepped toward the trail.

He didn't move aside to let her pass. He just stood under the sign, blocking the path's entrance. The wind chilled suddenly and smelled of roses. Realizing she was still clad in her white cotton nightgown, Margo started to wrap her arms around herself for warmth and thumped her hip with the yellow vinyl suitcase she held in her right hand.

Where had that come from?

She glanced from the suitcase to the strange man. "Am I dreaming?"

He shook his head, lifting the suitcase from her hand. "Hope you packed plenty of clothes."

"I … I didn't pack anything. I'm … I was in a fire."

He sobered a bit. "Yes, Margo, you were."

"You know who I am. How do you know who I am? I have no idea who— You're not *God*?"

"No, though I suspect some of the women I've known might disagree about that." He winked. "I'm Thomas. Thomas Tew."

"Thomas … the pirate?

"No longer. Now I'm just Thomas the Guide."

Sudden alarm threatened to swamp Margo's disorientation. "Guide to what?" She glanced up at the sign above Thomas's head. "Halfway? What's Halfway? Halfway to what?"

"All in God's time," he declared, as the corners of his lips curled upward slightly. This time, the smile failed to reach his eyes.

"Look, I think there's been some sort of mistake."

"So say you all. Tell me, darling girl, how do you feel?"

"I feel amazing, that's what's so weird. I was supposed to leave the party tonight with Eddie, but he left with Amy and I … I got caught in a fire. And I feel … pretty good."

"Ah, yes. The would-be boyfriend—Eddie. Close your eyes, take my hand."

"What, like in *A Christmas Carol*?"

"If you wish."

She closed her eyes and took the offered hand warily, feeling instantly warmed as his fingers intertwined with hers. A frisson of excitement rushed through her body as she transported out of herself.

"I believe you would call this a 'cool' view?" Thomas observed, pointing to the sun just appearing on the eastern horizon.

Margo couldn't disagree. They stood in the lee of the lighthouse on Rose Island, gazing toward the still-sleeping town of Newport, which spread out before them in panorama—roads, stores, houses, and gardens rising out of blue shadow into golden daylight. The waters of the bay lapped against the docks and kissed the hulls of the boats dotting its surface. The sky went from lavender to blue and the clouds on the horizon blushed at the first touch of the sun.

Thomas led her over the rocks and up the steep sandy slope to the door at the base of the old lighthouse. The climb seemed easier than she remembered. In fact, she wasn't panting even a little when they reached the crest.

A sign on the door read, "Went to town. Back at two o'clock."

Margo knew, now, that the keeper would not likely be back at 2:00 any day soon. The lighthouse hadn't been in regular service for years. Its future would be as a historical landmark to tour. She experienced a creeping sense of *deja vu* as Thomas tried the door. She knew it would open easily.

"Anybody here?" Thomas called mockingly, but his voice echoed off the walls of the ancient building. Just as Eddie's had, once.

No reply. Margo expected none.

They ascended the winding wrought iron staircase to the observation deck, enclosed by wraparound windows. Above their heads the huge rotating lamp at the top of the lighthouse lay dormant. They crossed to the far side of the deck where an old wooden door opened onto the living quarters of the lighthouse keeper.

Standing inside the small square space, they took in the lighthouse keeper's home, including the neatly made cot, the maple desk covered in nautical charts, and the row of hooks hung with yellow rain slickers and flashlights. On the floor a pair of galoshes awaited their owner. It looked just as it had the day she and Eddie had come here.

"Oh look, there's a cot. Sit down and make yourself comfortable." Thomas gestured. "Don't worry, I won't try anything funny … not yet, at least." He arched his eyebrows and laughed.

Had Eddie laughed? Memory said he had. Now she was supposed to continue … "This is the lighthouse keeper's bedroom. I don't think we should be in here."

"Trust me. He'll never know we were here." Thomas's eyes mocked.

Somehow having this … what was he, anyway? A spirit? An angel? A pirate ghost? She might have giggled at that idea, except this surreal replay of her visit here with Eddie made her soul writhe. Suddenly, she didn't feel so great.

She turned around to look at Thomas. Something enigmatic behind his eyes drew her in and repelled her at the same time. She tried to shake off her disorientation.

Margo told him, "This is the Rose Island lighthouse. I came here with Eddie. I don't know why we're reenacting … that time, but I know I'm dead. Am I the only one who didn't make it out of the fire?" She sounded so whiny, she cringed.

Thomas dropped his gaze. When he met her eyes again, he wore a more solemn expression than she'd yet seen. "You arrived with nine other girls from Francis Hall: Gina, Anya, the three track stars, and the four cheerleaders. They are visiting their own sacred places on Earth." He smiled briefly. "An interesting and diverse array."

Nine? Nine other girls had died with her in the fire? She felt as if gravity were suddenly drawing her toward the center of the Earth.

"I need some air."

It was a stupid thing to say under the circumstances, she supposed, but it was all she could think of. She walked out onto the observation deck. The fog, which had swaddled the base of the lighthouse, unwrapped the structure as if on cue, clearing a wide area around the tiny island.

Looking down, Margo observed three people sitting in a small dinghy just at the base of the rock, gazing up at her. One busily took notes. All were dressed alike in loose black robes cinched at the waist with white rope. Their oversized hoods made it difficult to tell if they were men or women. One of them waved.

"Who are they?" Margo asked Thomas, who had followed her out onto the deck.

"That's the Soul Cleansing Board. They're waiting to tell you about the Cross-over process. But I can give it to you in a nutshell. You're in Halfway. It's a semi-spirit state between the material world and Heaven. I'm your guide. Your ultimate goal is the Light ... the desire of all souls, the holy grail, I guess you'd say." He smiled wryly.

"So, I, what do I have to do to ... cross over?"

"That depends on you. On all of you."

"Wait. You told me I was the leader of the group. Are you talking about the ten of us—the ones killed in the fire?"

"Yes, though you're only bound to Gina. The other girls ... have different paths to tread. You're their leader because you went back for them. Tried to save them."

Man, Margo thought, things were growing weirder by the minute. She stood in a decommissioned lighthouse with a piratical spirit guide, while a monkish committee floated around in a dinghy, taking notes. How could that be real?

It also struck her as an ironic coincidence that she and Eddie had taken a boat named after her spirit guide on their visit to the lighthouse. Could she be dreaming, or having a near-death-experience? She prayed she was dreaming, because if not, Gina and eight of their dorm mates were dead, too.

Skeptical, she asked, "So why don't we just all cross over now? What are we waiting for?"

"In your case," Thomas explained, "you can only cross over when you and Gina are both ready. The Soul Cleansing Board makes that determination."

In my case? What did that mean?

She had too many questions. So she picked one. "What do you mean when you say 'ready'?"

"Some spirits don't cross over—at least not right away," Thomas told her. "It's almost impossible to cross over immediately when your death is unexpected, which is why all ten of you will need some time to process what's happened. When and if you do accept the suddenness of it all, you may be blocked from moving on for other reasons. For example, I suspect you're thinking that this is a dream."

Margo glanced at him, startled.

He shrugged. "Indeed, that happens often. The denial of the dead. Then again, some spirits are too attached to something or someone in the physical world that they feel they cannot leave.

The most difficult spirit to cross over is one who is harboring remorse. That's a tough one."

Was his gaze just a bit too intense? Why? She regretted that she and Eddie hadn't been able to have a real relationship, but remorse? No. That wasn't her fault, after all. What did she have to be remorseful about?

Light dawned slowly. Gina: he must be talking about Gina and her chaotic, intermittent relationship with Carlos.

"What if one of us is ready to cross over and the other isn't?" Margo asked.

"Both of you will be held back," Thomas replied. "There's a compromise solution though. If the Soul Cleansing Board sees this is the situation, they will allow the one who is ready to cross over temporary access to the Light. Of course, they must return to Halfway when it's night in the part of the world they're from. It's not ideal, but it's the way of things here."

"You mean, it's like we'd get a visitor's pass to hang out with God?"

Thomas laughed, a free, boisterous sound becoming a pirate. "I suppose you could put it that way. When the physical light fades on your earthly home, you would return to Halfway."

"Why?"

"God works in mysterious ways. We can't always understand the laws of divine physics."

Margo nodded. She suspected arguing the laws of divine physics would be much like disputing the mundane ones. In a knock-down-drag-out fight with gravity, gravity always wins. She suspected she now knew that firsthand.

A sudden, whimsical thought struck Margo. "Is that why ghosts do their haunting at night?"

Thomas laughed again, then turned to wave to the people

below them in the dinghy. "Ahoy!" he shouted. "Margo is as bright as she is lovely. She's catching on."

She'd caught on to something else too, though belatedly. "The lighthouse is my sacred place?"

Thomas's gaze turned to her again, full of wry humor. "Apparently."

"Why?"

"Only you know the answer to that one. It's *your* sacred place."

She thought about it and didn't like what her thoughts suggested. This was her sacred place because she'd had sex here with Eddie? Was she really that shallow?

No, she wasn't. "I loved Eddie."

Thomas shrugged. "Rings true. Sacred places almost always have something to do with love. You probably still love Eddie."

She squared her spectral shoulders and ignored that probability. "So, the lighthouse is my sacred place. Great. Where do I go next?"

"Where do you feel you should go?"

Suddenly, she felt the pull of her physical body. "Where am I? I mean, where's my—you know—my body?" She couldn't bring herself to say "corpse."

"It's been taken to the hospital nearest the school."

"That's where my family will be. Where Eddie will be … right?"

Thomas held out his hand again and she took it.

There was a waiting room just down the broad hospital hall from the emergency room's intake. From it, Margo could see the strobe lights of ambulances flashing along the floor.

Was that her ambulance, Margo wondered? Surely not. Surely she was already here in some room or alcove. The fire had been hours ago, now. Her body might already be in the morgue. Or maybe she rested unconscious in a regular room, having a horrible dream.

No, she lay in an admitting room with an oxygen mask still covering her face, blood matting her hair, and the heart monitor standing, silent, beside her gurney. She knew it with absolute certainty, but shoved the knowledge away as she searched the crowded waiting room for her mom and dad among the other grief-stricken families.

She found them easily. They were huddled by the television set nested in one corner. It was probably there to distract the waiting room occupants from what was happening in the ER just yards away. But she watched her mother flipping through one station after another, stopping at each news report, raising the volume over the chaos in the room.

Early morning sunlight crept in through the slats of the horizontal blinds, painting bright stripes across the linoleum of the waiting room floor. One of the stripes lay across the toes of her dad's shoes. He studied its progress over his shoelaces. With his red-rimmed eyes and sagging face, dad looked centuries old. A nearly empty bottle of soda dangled from his listless fingers.

Her mom changed channels again.

"Agnes, please!" The cry came from a woman at the center of another family group—the mother of one of the cheerleaders, Margo thought. "Turn it off! How can you stand to hear them—" The woman covered her ears with her hands and began to weep.

"For God sake, Agnes, stop!" Gyp exclaimed, reaching out to pull his wife's hand from the channel knob. "You're making it worse."

He snapped the TV off.

Agnes gave her husband a fierce glare of equal parts despair and rage. "How can I possibly make it worse?" she shuddered.

Margo drew closer to them, sitting in the seat next to her mom, feeling her heart constrict, as if squeezed in a vise. She was vaguely surprised that she could sit in a physical chair.

"Mom," she tried to comfort her. "Mom, I'm okay. I'm all right." She reached out a hand toward her mother, but Thomas stopped her with a shake of his head.

"You can't touch her. It will leave an imprint. Best you not handle objects either." He slanted a glance at the chair Margo sat in.

She stood as if the chair had burned her, watching as her mom turned a hungry gaze to the blank television screen.

"I feel … like she's still out there," Agnes Tracey murmured.

"I am, Mom!"

"She can't hear you," whispered Thomas quietly. "We're … out of phase with their reality."

Gyp spoke again, his hand in his wife's. "Those talking heads can't tell you anything about Margo, Agnes. Only the people at this hospital can tell us anything about Margo now."

"I was hoping …"

"I know what you were hoping," Gyp responded gently. "That you might see her there, sitting in an ambulance, talking to a reporter. But you're not going to see that because she's here, in the hospital. We saw them bring her in."

"It might have been someone else, Gyp," Agnes wailed, desperation clotting her voice. "We only saw her for a second—"

A grey-haired doctor in a white coat came into the room just then. He paused to look at all the faces turned toward him, then walked over to Margo's parents. He had a kind face; a tired face; a sad face.

"I'm sorry, but we were unable to revive your daughter. There was simply too much damage. She's just down the hall. Would you like to see her, now?"

Agnes' voice failed her. She just blinked. Blinked and glanced at the TV set as if it might make a lie of the doctor's words.

Gyp set his soda bottle down on a side table and nodded. "Yes, doctor, thank you."

The doctor shook his head. "I wish to God I *could* give you something to thank me for, but …"

He helped Gyp get Agnes to her feet then flagged down a nurse and instructed her to take Margo's parents to their daughter.

But I'm not there, anymore, Margo thought, and wondered why she couldn't *feel* what she knew she should. Her parents were crumbling before her eyes and she could only feel a sort of deep emotional bruising. Nothing like what she knew she'd experience if one of them had died and left her.

But you're the one who's left them behind.

"Do you want to go with them?" Thomas asked.

She shook her head. She didn't want to see her own body. She didn't want…. She looked down at her hands—held them out in front of her.

"I know my body is … down there somewhere." She tilted her head toward the hall. "So, what is this? Is this a-a celestial body?"

She'd read about those in the Bible and heard numerous sermons about them. One of her evangelical friends called them "glorified" bodies. Clad in a white cotton nightgown and barefoot, she felt neither glorified or celestial.

"It's a Halfway body. It's … what you make of it."

Moments later, Margo stood in the doorway of Eddie's dorm room. Amy sat cross-legged at the foot of Eddie's bed while he was across the room, bouncing his basketball against the wall behind her. His high-tops and dirty uniform lay in a pile on the floor next to his dresser and a laundry basket filled with dirty clothes.

What a slob, Margo thought, as an overwhelming feeling of affection for him welled in her chest. He was crying. Margo had never seen Eddie cry, not even when his father had punched him.

Amy shifted uncomfortably on the bed. "Why don't we go to Dempsey's for some breakfast? You have to eat, and getting out of here might do us some good." Her voice pleaded softly.

Eddie let the ball drop and turned his tear-stained face to Amy. "The ladder was four feet away, Amy. The firefighters were working on getting it closer, on sending up an extension. Why didn't she hear me yelling for her to hang tight? Why didn't she hear the fireman? He was so close." He reached out a hand as if he could touch the imaginary Margo and draw her to safety.

"I didn't see the ladder," Margo murmured. "I heard someone shouting, but I didn't see the ladder." She raised her own spectral hand, almost touching Eddie's fingertips. Thomas stopped her, shaking his head.

"She had already inhaled so much smoke, Eddie," Amy consoled him. "Even if she'd … even if she'd survived the fall, we can't be sure she wouldn't have died from the smoke."

"She was so smart, why would she jump?"

"Maybe she didn't feel she had a choice. Or maybe she didn't jump; maybe she fell."

"The fireman thought it looked like they jumped."

Margo shook her head. "I didn't mean to jump, Eddie. You have to believe me."

Eddie's face twisted in grief. "If only they had seen the ladder … the goddamn ladder was *so close*."

"Do they … do they even know what caused it, yet?"

Eddie shook his head. "Not really. They know it started in the fourth floor bathroom. The fire marshall reported there was a lot of stuff plugged into the sockets—hair dryers and stuff.

Could have been an electrical short. Could've been somebody left a hairdryer on..."

A hairdryer? They might've been killed by a hairdryer that someone left on?

"Why would somebody leave a damn hairdryer on, anyway?" Eddie asked, anger and pain blending in his voice.

Amy shrugged. "We sometimes used them to dry damp clothes. Margo showed us how to prop one up and..." Her voice went all wobbly. "Margo was so clever."

Margo felt as if the world had stopped turning. Clever Margo used a hairdryer to dry damp clothes. Clever Margo. Had clever Margo used a hairdryer that night? She tried, but couldn't remember. She thought to ask Thomas, but couldn't make herself even think the words.

"God, Eddie," Amy cried, "why am *I* still alive? If I hadn't been with you, I wouldn't be. *Margo* was the one who was going to make history; I can barely pass my classes. None of this makes any sense. I feel like I'm having a nightmare and Gina and Margo are going to wake me for class soon."

The uncertainty and fear that had enveloped Margo swiftly morphed into anger. She loomed over Amy, though she knew the other girl couldn't see her.

"You're right, Amy—I *was* going to make history. How am I supposed to do it now, in the lovely hereafter, with Captain Hook following me around giving me orders? *I* was supposed to be in Eddie's room that night, not you."

Margo collapsed to the floor in tears. *It was supposed to be me. He was supposed to be with me.*

Eddie came to the bed and put his hand to Amy's cheek, almost brushing Margo's hair. Then he crossed the room to his desk, fumbled through a messy pile of schedules, notes, and arena tickets. He came up with the ring, his lucky ring, and cradled it in his fingers.

"I gave this to Margo once and she gave it back to me." Eddie wiped at his wet face with the back of his hand. "It's my sophomore year championship ring. Brings me good luck. I was gonna give it back to Margo when the time was right."

Eddie placed it gently in the palm of Amy's hands and closed her fist tightly bringing her hand up to his lips for a kiss.

Margo crawled on her hands and knees toward them. *Please don't give it to Amy.*

"This is a weird time to ask me to go steady, Eddie Sullivan," Amy responded.

"I think Margo would be happy if you had it." His voice broke into a sob, "It'll be like the ring is back in the game in some way."

Margo shot up in a blast to the ceiling and back to the floor, letting out a high-pitched wail. She barely registered that she could now defy the law of gravity. "How the hell would you know what makes me happy? How do you know how this would make me feel! Do you even care?"

Margo's throat burned and her eyes stung as she fought back tears. Then Tew's hand touched her arm.

"Not much better here?" Thomas asked.

She shook her head, not trusting herself to speak without crying. "Time's up, Red. Gina will be needing you."

* * *

Carlos Delgado used a fan brush to apply splashes of gold to the trees that formed the landscape background on a large canvas. The easel took center stage in his studio; completed and half-finished canvases were stacked against two walls.

From where Gina stood in the archway connecting to the next room, she could make out a figure in the foreground of the painting. Though only pencil lines defined the face, Gina realized it was the nude portrait of her that Carlos had started before they broke up.

Carlos's hair looked wet, as if he'd just showered. She moved closer to him and inhaled, smelling his shampoo, the fresh musk of his skin. She suddenly felt how much she wanted him.

I was so stupid. How could I have let him go?

She heard the steady beat of his heart. Magnified senses. She wondered how she'd even arrived here. Hadn't she just been in her dorm room? Her last memory struggled to surface—their dorm room last night after the Blind Date Ball. There had been some sort of excitement. Her mind lunged after the vague memory, but she harnessed it.

Carlos stared over the partially completed nude portrait shaking his head. He reached for his palette, mixing the different colors with the tip of his brush.

"Damn you, Carlos Delgado. What the hell are you doing? I told you not to paint me, and I meant it. You have a new girlfriend. Why don't you paint her?"

He stood back from the painting a bit, then began applying broad strokes to the canvas. He didn't so much as glance at her.

"I'm talking to you. Don't ignore me, you—you moron! And tell me just how the hell you managed to get the night of the Blind Date Ball wrong, huh? You couldn't even get the freaking date right for the damn dance! Some kind of artistic genius you are--one who can't read a calendar!"

She stopped, trembling. *Why won't he look at me?*

In all of their twisted history, Carlos had *never* given her the silent treatment. He was a confronter, a negotiator, a placater.

He hated unresolved issues, whereas Gina viewed certainty as a straightjacket. Maybe that was why things were so screwed up between them.

Carlos sighed, put down his brush and left the room. His shoulders sagged as if in defeat.

As if I were a disappointment to HIM, Gina thought, angrily. For a split second she contemplated destroying the painting, but wasn't willing to go that far. She settled for grabbing a piece of pottery from a shelf full of student projects and hurling it at the wall. It shattered satisfyingly, one piece almost hitting Margo, who gazed at her from the archway. Behind Margo, in the foyer, Carlos paused and glanced back over his shoulder. The jerk ignored Margo, too.

Gina hesitated, confused. What was Margo doing here ... wearing a nightgown? The thoughts had no more than occurred to her than Margo hurried into the studio and snatched at her hands. She looked down, realizing that she'd picked up another piece of pottery—a mug with a heart on it.

"Don't touch things, Gina. We're not supposed to touch things. Or people."

"What are you talking about? What do you mean we're not supposed to touch things? And why are you still wearing your nightgown?"

The despondent look on Margo's face almost made Gina burst into tears.

"Oh, Gina, it's..." She stopped. "What do you remember about last night?"

"I remember that stupid Carlos got the night of the ball wrong and stood me up and—and..."

Margo gently put the mug back on the shelf and took Gina's hands in her own. "That wasn't his fault. I think it was mine.

I may have told him it was Saturday instead of Friday. *Think*, Gina. What else do you remember ... about after the dance?"

She shrugged. "We went back to the dorm. I wanted to meet Carlos—who stood me up."

Margo looked as if she were going to cry. "Oh, Gina, no—he didn't stand you up. You never went to meet him. There was—"

"A fire," Gina chimed in unison with her.

She remembered. The smell of smoke, fleeing to the corridor, Margo turning back to make sure no one in the corner rooms got left behind. Being trapped in the cheerleaders' room with no way out. *Except down.*

No. It wasn't possible. Gina bent down and tried to pick up the pieces of shattered pottery.

"Forget it," Margo called, tugging at her arm. "We have to go."

"Says who?"

"Our guide. He's here somewhere. He brought me to you. His name is Thomas."

"Our guide? Our guide for what?" She felt woozy suddenly. Migraine aura. Damn. She put a hand to her head. "My head is gonna be splitting in just a moment. I feel a migraine coming on."

"I don't think you can have migraines anymore," Margo told her. "Look at me, Gina. I'm wearing my nightgown because it's what I wore last night. *My* last night. *Our* last night. I died in this clothing, Gina."

Gina took a step back. Had Margo completely lost her mind? Worse, had Gina lost hers as well? Because she remembered the fire now. The panic, the pain, the air being eaten by the flames until there was no oxygen left for the ten girls trapped in the dorm room to breathe.

137

She stumbled to the mirror that ran the length of the back wall of the studio, her eyes on her own reflection. The right side of her face burned black, the skin curling and splitting away from her skull. One side of her mouth curled up in a deathly grin, exposing her teeth all the way back to her molars. Her beautiful hair half gone and what remained singed in a frizzy mat. Her right eyebrow vaporized.

She reached up with her fingers patted the swollen surface of her cheek. No sensation. In the mirror, she could see that her hands were horribly burned as well. She let out a wail of terror.

"Why? Why am I like this?"

Margo came up behind her, frowning. "Like what?"

"I've been cooked, damnit! I'm grotesque!"

"No. No you're not."

Gina touched her face again. "I'm burned!"

Margo shook her head. "You look normal to me—but in your nightgown."

Gina swung back to the mirror. The nightgown had partially melted and melded with the skin over her right hip. She didn't understand why Margo didn't see her that way, but it didn't matter. This was what she was now. No physical pain, but emotional anguish beyond endurance.

She turned away from the mirror and sank to the floor, wrapping her arms around her knees. The things she valued the most—Carlos and her sexuality—were gone.

Margo knelt down and squeezed Gina's hand. "Come on," she prodded, "It's time to go."

Margo led her to the sidewalk in front of the fine arts building. Their guide —Thomas — met them. Gina registered his good looks vaguely—his sexiness, in his billowing shirt and tight pants.

"He looks like a pirate," she whispered to Margo.

"He *is* a pirate. Or, rather, he was. He's been dead a long time."

Thomas smiled at them. "Ready to go back to Halfway?"

"Halfway," Gina repeated. She recognized it, which surprised her, though less than closing her eyes standing in front of the fine arts building at RIT and opening them in a glade vibrating with super-real colors surrounded by a picture postcard wood.

"I'll see you soon," Thomas assured them, as he headed away toward the woods. "You may want to change your clothes."

"Change my clothes?" Gina repeated shrilly. "I want to change my *skin*! I'm—I'm a wreck!"

Thomas stopped and turned to look her up and down. "Listen," he replied, smiling. "All that is up to you." He turned away again and walked off, whistling, disappearing before he reached the edge of the wood.

10

February, 1978

THEIR LITTLE "ISLAND" IN Halfway was roughly circular and outfitted with a waterfall that cascaded into a clear pool with a cluster of crystalline rocks poking above its surface. The ambient light made rainbows in the mist. Margo wasn't certain why this place existed; she wasn't even sure she and Gina experienced it in the same way as they perched on the rocks, waiting in a figurative line for a visit to the physical world.

Margo had been hovering on the fringes of Halfway every afternoon since that day she went with Thomas to see her parents and Eddie. Her first scheduled lab meeting with fellow Science Club spirits for CHP would take place next week at 3:00 AM sharp. She didn't want that to be her first earthly visit since her death.

So far, she had found everything she needed here within arm's reach. Her dorm room looked so much like Francis 405 that she felt completely at home. Her small circle of friends in Halfway contained Gina and the eight other girls from Francis

Hall, including several pre-med and science track students, and a few other nerdy-type spirits. She hadn't joined in on the Halfway "island-hopping" (or "cloud-hopping" as some of the denizens of Halfway insisted on calling it). Thomas lived on what he liked to call the Pirate Cloud and, while Margo wasn't opposed to stopping by his place if she had a question on protocol or rules, she rarely needed to visit because he always seemed to be close by the moment she thought of him. Though aloof, he responded when questioned. Margo sensed his mind wandered somewhere else.

In the moment she became aware their turn had arrived and she felt Gina's hand on her shoulder.

"Is today the day, Margo?"

"As good a day as any," Margo confirmed, with more confidence than she felt. She took Gina's hand, knowing Gina had been itching to try her first earth bound visit, but feared traveling alone. "We'll dive together."

"I'm going to Carlos's apartment," Gina declared.

"I'm visiting CHP. I'll come find you later."

Margo had always loved winter, and they'd picked an ideal morning for building snowmen. The kind of morning where freshly fallen snow blanketed the ground and gave the living the impression that everything under it could be erased. Margo dug her bare feet into the snow. Though aware of the cold, she couldn't feel it, even though she still wore only her nightgown.

January had blustered in with a blizzard of epic proportions hitting Rhode Island during the night, leaving it in a state of emergency. The cars in the Francis Hall parking lot looked like vague humps of snow. The silence was broken only by the biting clang of the snow shovel against asphalt, where a groundskeeper worked at the opposite side of the lot, trying to clear a narrow pathway. A tiny white whirlwind of snow blew past, lifting Margo's long red curls from her shoulders.

Margo stared up at the fourth floor window of Francis Hall, searching for evidence of the fire. Though the thick snowflakes obscured her vision, it appeared as if all traces of the fire had been erased, except for the telltale soot-blackened bricks above the window.

The dorm's front door opened and a stream of students emerged. Bundled up in parkas, boots, hats, and gloves, they walked single file on the narrowly shoveled path. A few threw snowballs, but for the most part, they seemed focused on getting somewhere in a hurry. Margo drifted along behind them, curious and unhampered by the snow.

The group expanded as more students and faculty headed down the path toward the Yarmouth Street gate where a yellow school bus waited with an escort—a police car in front and a fire truck behind, lights flashing.

Margo waited until the basketball team had boarded the bus, then slipped in past the team's center, chatting with his teammates; the coach, studying a play book and making notes to himself; and the cheerleaders, dressed in white turtlenecks and short pleated skirts, resting their pompoms on their laps.

Margo spotted Eddie hunched in the back of the bus staring moodily out at the snow. She glided down the aisle and sat down next to him. His sulky expression didn't surprise her, but she thought she detected something behind his patented "I don't care" attitude, something anxious and vulnerable behind his smooth facade. She felt a rush of emotion and reached out a hand to brush the hair back from his forehead, then froze. She wasn't going to fail at Haunting 101. No movements, no touching, no attempts to communicate—but, oh God, how she wanted to kiss him.

Just a soft kiss, just the barest brushing of her lips against his.

Then she remembered Amy. She clenched her fist, banging it down on the worn vinyl seat. "I bet Amy will bring you good luck tonight," she snarled.

Eddie brushed his errant forelock from his forehead, then folded his arms across his chest and scowled down at the floor.

The bus driver started the engine and pulled onto the street, while the crowd of students waved and cheered, following in the wake of the team bus. As the bus ground its way down Yarmouth Street, Margo looked up and observed the coach standing in the aisle peering down at Eddie.

"How's the knee?" he asked.

"Not so good. It hurts." Eddie didn't look up.

"I'm having second thoughts about even having you play," the coach remarked.

Eddie's expression turned fierce. "The mayor opened the airport just to fly in the Hartford Tech team, Coach. And we need this win. Me sitting on the bench isn't an option. I mean ... look outside."

They both looked out the window. Margo followed their gazes and saw the droves of people walking alongside the bus as if on a religious pilgrimage. More were funneling in to join the throng as if a bus filled with scrappy basketball players carried a savior or a king.

"I know, son," the coach tried to reassure him. "This is pressure. After the fire, those poor girls and their families ... the school—hell, the *city*—needs a win. When I think about that night..." His voice cracked.

Margo watched as Eddie flinched and paled before he resumed his mask of careful nonchalance.

"Well, if they need a win, we'll just have to deliver it for them," he pledged.

"An injury?" Margo asked, leaning in dangerously close to his face. "I told you this was the reason you needed to actually get an education."

Eddie bit his lip and pulled his hoodie up as if he were trying to escape from her—or from his own thoughts.

"Well, don't come crying to me when you can't play ball anymore," Margo snapped, but a sob caught in her throat. How could he come to her at all anymore? He was on his own. She couldn't help him now.

* * *

Gina soaked in the big old claw-footed tub in Carlos's apartment, white washcloth folded and covering her eyes. Soaking had been the only remedy for the migraines she suffered since she had been a kid. Even now they comforted her, though she only imagined she could feel the water's heat. It didn't matter. She would wait for Carlos for as long as it took. She had nowhere else to go. He had to come home sometime.

As she heard the door open, she smothered the soap in the washcloth and feverishly scrubbed the burns up to her elbows and the red bubbling open wounds on her palms and forearms. *I'm a damn circus freak*, she thought. She continued to scrub, then looked up.

Margo stood in the doorway. "Come to the Civic Center with me for the basketball game, like you did that time last year."

"I can't. I'm busy." Gina spoke through the ghost of pain in her head.

"You're going to spend your first earthly visits swimming in Carlos's bathtub?"

"Why not?" Gina asked.

"I heard bits and pieces on the CHP basketball bus. It's an important game. We should be there."

"It's a *basketball* game, Margo," replied Gina caustically. "CHP meant nothing to me when I attended. A bunch of uptight girls pretending to be virgins—what were they trying to prove? Remember that girl who used to work the front desk at Francis? I used to come in some mornings in the same clothes I had on the night before and she would give me this look like 'what kind of whore are you?' As if her pussy was better than mine because she kept it locked up in some kind of CHP chastity belt."

"I always wondered why she didn't report you," mused Margo.

Gina made a face. "I gave her stuff. Perfume, jewelry, makeup."

"Come out of the tub. But don't take a towel. We are not supposed to touch anything," Margo reminded her, "and you've already touched plenty."

Gina stood. "I'll touch what I want." She stepped out of the tub, reached for the white towel that hung on the back of the door, and wrapped it around her chest, tucking in the ends.

"Now you've done it, "Margo warned. "Not only are you touching things, you're using linens."

Gina looked at the medicine chest mirror and leaned forward. "Look at me. Do you think I could get a guy on our cloud to even take me out for a walk, never mind out for a night of mind-blowing sex?" She tipped her head back and let out a joyless laugh.

"You still look sexy to me," Margo soothed her.

Gina opened the medicine chest, reached in and found a pair of scissors on the bottom shelf next to a messy bottle of shaving cream and rusted nail clippers. She held the edge of the blade against her index finger.

"Stop!" Margo implored, her voice rising in panic. "You're going too far. If Thomas hears about this, he may not let us come back."

"I haven't gone too far yet. But I'm going to in a minute." Gina raised the scissors in one hand and a bunch of her hair in the other. With the precision she applied to painting, she cut in fast wild clips. Clumps of her long black hair fell to the tiled floor, the wisps scattering around her feet.

"Stop!" Margo cried again, frozen in the doorway.

Gina ignored her and kept cutting, her eyes darting wildly.

Her task complete, Gina stared at her close-cropped reflection in the mirror. "Now this style suits the rest of me—repulsive. Who needs long flowing hair? No man is ever going to want me. No man is going to feel my hair brushing his face when we—"

"Come with me," Margo begged. "Please, Gina. Let's leave. Right now."

Gina sank to her knees and began to finger the tendrils of hair littering the floor. *A failed first visit*, she thought. *Maybe it was for the best.*

She stretched out one arm and Margo caught it, pulling Gina to her feet.

"I just gave myself a crew cut and Carlos may never come home tonight for all I know." She put her head on Margo's shoulder. "Have it your way. Let's go to the game."

* * *

Inside, the noise flowed over the crowded arena as spectators took programs, brought popcorn and found their seats.

Margo led Gina along the bleachers down to the floor. "Let's sit right behind the bench."

147

"Sure, so you can drool at Eddie's ass in his tight shorts and I can file my nails," an exasperated Gina remarked.

Margo fixed her gaze on the CHP team. Eddie gave a pump up talk to his huddled team in front of their bench. She longed to hear the sound of his voice.

At center court, the Governor of Rhode Island strode out to a small platform, tapped on the mike, then cleared his throat. The fans perked up.

"What is he saying?" Gina asked.

"I can hardly hear him. I can make out only a few words." Margo strained to listen. "I'm only getting bits and pieces. Thomas warned me this might happen. It's because we're out of phase with the physical world. I think he's talking about what it will mean to Rhode Island if CHP beats the undefeated team from Hartford Tech."

"Why would the state care?" Gina wondered. "It's just another basketball game."

"He's saying it matters because the state of Rhode Island is in mourning."

"Over what?" Gina asked.

"Us, Gina. The Governor is talking about us—you, me, the cheerleaders, the runners. Darn it, why can't I make out what he's saying?"

Margo wished she could hear clearly to catch one announcement she expected the Governor to make. She closed her eyes and imagined what the Governor *should* say: "Ladies and Gentlemen, we now know the cause of the fire. Well, you'll hardly believe this, but the same straight-A student destined to be your state's first female surgeon caused the blaze. Drying wet clothes with a hairdryer. She thought she was so clever. Everyone described her as so clever."

Red Mittens

Margo opened her eyes. The spectators in the stands weeped. She scanned for Eddie and found him sitting on the bench, his head buried in his towel, his shoulders shaking.

The Governor continued his speech, pointing to ten color photo banners hanging from the rafters. Candid shots of the ten girls. Draped in the center was Margo, wearing a white lab coat and bent over a microscope. To her left hung a photo of Gina posed in a plié on the CHP theatre stage. To her right, a shot of Anya, her short blonde hair in twin pony tails and a dab of paint on her nose. Margo remembered—it had been taken when they'd made banners for a homecoming dance. A shot of the four cheerleaders showed each as part of a human pyramid, huge smiles on their faces. The three runners were shown in shots taken at track meets—on the track or on the awards platform.

Margo put her arm around Gina and whispered in her ear, "Look at the pictures. You belonged here as much as anyone else—lousy haircut and all."

Gina laughed again, this time a wild laugh, laced with hysteria. Margo envied her roommate's reckless disregard for composure.

Gina cocked her head back. "If you say so."

Margo watched her face as Gina took in the banners and the tears in the spectators' eyes. Remembering.

* * *

Eddie applauded along with everyone else when the Governor finished his speech. His heart raced, his hands shook. Strange, he thought. He never felt nervous before a game. He rubbed his knee and tried to breathe steadily. Screw the pain, he cursed silently, then took his position on the court.

Minutes before halftime, as Eddie drove toward the basket, an opponent's block from his right forced him sharply left. White-hot pain seared through his knee. He went down hard on the boards, clutching his left knee.

Eddie could tell something was wrong—really wrong. He held in his cries as the trainer rushed onto the court. The crowd quieted. When the trainer flexed his knee, it took every ounce of Eddie's strength to suppress a scream. The paramedics joined the trainer on the court. The crowd applauded as the medics lifted him onto a stretcher and carried him off the court.

Inside the locker room, Eddie lay stiffly on his back on the exam table, trying to relax. Taking Eddie's knee in both hands, the trainer bent it toward Eddie's stomach, then moved it clockwise in slow circular motions. He continued the rotation a few times then released it.

"What's the story?" Eddie demanded through gritted teeth.

"I don't know, "the trainer looked him in the eye. "I paged the orthopedic surgeon. We'll have to see what he says."

Eddie held the bag of ice against his swollen knee and kicked off his sneakers. *Screw the trainer,* he cursed to himself. Now, he'd have to wait to hear what the orthopedic surgeon had to say. That meant x-rays. It meant he wouldn't be allowed back on the court. He knew the trainer had already done everything he could for his knee; he'd iced and wrapped it, given Eddie an over-the-counter painkiller. If the knee needed surgery, he might just have to kiss his professional career goodbye.

He closed his eyes and tried to think. That he might never be drafted by the NBA occurred to him for the very first time. He'd been so damned certain. He'd been on an unstoppable hot streak. Jesus—could this really be happening?

Margo's warnings about the risk of being injured weighed on his thoughts.

Damn her. Damn her for being right.

* * *

Margo watched as the surgeon entered the examination room in the ER and took a seat on the stool by Eddie's side. She didn't have to hear the conversation to know the gravity of the news the surgeon delivered to Eddie. She watched his reaction, the way his face tightened in pain, and she burst into tears, holding her hands to her face. She became aware of the surgeon's briefcase, dropped on the floor next to the table. Margo moved to get a closer look at the newspaper protruding from the outside flap. The headline read, "Grieving students hope for a win." The column below enlarged on the theme: "Grieving students hope for a win in today's game against undefeated Hartford Technical. After the recent fire in Francis Hall at Christopher Hayes Prep..." The flap obscured the rest of the article.

Margo hesitated. It was a slight violation to move and touch things, but nothing as dire as altering a mortal's destiny. Slowly, she extended her hand, reaching for the edge of the paper. It wouldn't hurt anyone if she just lifted it a little farther out, and Gina had done it...

Behind her, someone quietly cleared his throat. Margo turned and spied one of the Soul Cleansing Board members standing in a darkened corner, dressed in his uniform brown robe tied with a white rope. He shook his head as he jotted notes on his clipboard.

She looked back at the briefcase. Thomas materialized at her side.

"You've been doing so good today. Even helping Gina. Why ruin it now? What is it about the fire you need to know?"

"Nothing," she replied. "There's nothing I need to know."

"Let's go," Thomas instructed, and took her hand.

* * *

Night had descended on Thomas's Halfway cottage. He sat at the window of his bedroom in a white nightshirt, with a small glass of rum in one hand and a cigar in the other. They weren't real, of course, just affectations. It seemed even a spirit guide could have attachments to earthly things. He gazed out the window over moonlit clouds.

Margo stepped down into the sunken bedroom that had all the makings of a pirate museum: a wooden bed covered in a thick velvet bedspread, a treasure chest with copper and gold piled high, and faded maps stacked on an embroidered arm chair.

The last couple of times she had come with a question, she had found him in the captain's cabin aboard a pirate ship. Caught him with different women: bawdy pirate wenches who seemed made up out of some adventure tale. She wondered if they were spirits or just part of his set dressing. Tonight he rested alone in his Newport cottage. Tonight, he looked older and more worn. She sat down on the opposite end of the window bench.

Thomas lifted the bottle next to him and topped off his glass. "So, what brings you here?" he inquired, with a slightly drunken slur.

"I want to talk about this afternoon—you know, in the ER."

"What's there to talk about?" Thomas got up and walked to the corner table arranged with bottles of rum and glasses. He poured and passed a dusty glass to Margo.

She knew the stuff wasn't even real—or at least not physical. She didn't have the will to pretend it was. "Why did one of the Soul Cleansing Board members follow me in the locker room?" she asked, setting the glass down. It made no sound on the wood of the window sill. She hadn't expected it to.

"They were shadowing you to see how your (and Gina's) first solo visit went." He moved to stand by the window again, awkwardly smoothing his unruly hair. "They're getting ready to call your group in to see how you're all adjusting to ... things."

"So how'm I doing?" Margo asked.

"Today raised a red flag for me and for the Board," Thomas worried.

"You mean the thing with the newspaper?"

He nodded. "You were going along perfectly, gallivanting all over CHP as if you never left, hopping on the bus, then aiding Gina. Trying to keep her from a violation. A real Girl Scout of a ghost," Thomas remarked.

He drained his glass and flopped down onto his bed where he reached into the treasure chest and absently picked up a handful of gold. "Then," he continued, "your desire to read the newspaper article from the surgeon's briefcase exceeded the usual emotional reactions we often observe on earthly visits. You would have lifted that paper, if I hadn't saved you."

"I didn't need saving. I didn't need your help."

"Ah, yes," Thomas smirked. "I forgot. You're the lady who doesn't need any help or saving. You're the one who *does* the saving."

Margo looked away. *Stay focused.* "What do they care if I move the paper? What about Gina? She cut her hair in Carlos's apartment. How many demerits for that?"

"We're not talking about your friend's journey," Thomas explained.

"So it's okay for Gina to do whatever she wants."

"Gina's emotional landscape is different than yours. Her reaction is to be expected. There's more concern over you."

"Why?"

"What are you searching for?"

"Nothing, I told you."

"You're holding out on me," Thomas sighed. "It's going to surface eventually, but until it does, it may hold you back from crossing over."

"I don't know what you're talking about."

"I told you when we first met. The spirits who harbor hidden remorse are the toughest to cross over."

Margo tried not to react. "You're badgering the wrong ghost. I don't have any remorse. Go to Hell."

"Eventually, I'm sure I will. Why do you think I have no desire to cross over? I'm probably not going to the same place you're going."

No, Margo knew she'd be going to exactly the same place as Thomas. She didn't need a series of soul cleansing meetings to reveal her fate.

"I should go," Margo remarked, getting to her spirit feet.

"You and the others are going to have your first soul cleansing meeting and they are going to ask you the same things I'm asking you now. At some point, you will need to talk."

"What if I can't make the Board meeting? What if I'm busy? I mean, maybe I don't want them asking a bunch of questions," Margo scowled, cringing at the desperation in her voice.

"While you're figuring all of this out on your own, you might as well make your time here worthwhile. Put those academic talents of yours to good use." Thomas walked unsteadily over to the near-empty bottle of rum. "Go after what you want *here*."

"And what is it exactly you think I want here?" Margo asked. Realizing she found his affected drunkenness annoying.

"Advancement. Make a medical contribution in your science club—a cure for your father's alcoholism, say."

My father's alcoholism? What about yours? "I'm not a psychologist. I'm not into curing the mentally stressed. Drinking too much is an emotional problem, not medical," she added pointedly.

"Touché. Breakthrough surgery for your boyfriend's torn knee, then. You're the pre-med student, not me." He shuffled unsteadily over to the bed leaving a trail of cigar smoke and sat down.

Reaching for a portrait of a woman and a toddler that perched atop the bedside table, Thomas curved his fingers around the oval frame as he cradled it against his chest. He closed his eyes and lay back on the bed.

"I will never forget the sound of her playing her harp," he whispered, then began to snore.

Margo knelt over the bed and studied the photo. The way the young woman rested her hands affectionately on the little girl's shoulders suggested love. Margo began to understand that there might be more to Thomas Tew than rum, loose women and spectral dictatorship.

When she straightened, Margo noticed how the shirt's fabric collapsed over his abdomen, devoid of support. She couldn't help herself; she held her breath and pushed the shirt up, revealing a hollow hole the size of a cannonball in his lower abdomen.

She watched him sleep, wondering if that was just his way of avoiding dealing with her, noticing that he had lost the air of superiority he had when awake. She mused about the hole in his stomach, which history books attributed to the cannonball that killed him during his second voyage as a pirate. She questioned why he kept it. Did he have to, or did he choose to?

Except for that deformity, he seemed a normal man ... spirit, whatever. She tried to picture what he would have looked like in modern clothes—jeans and a polo shirt, say, or shorts and deck shoes. She smiled as she realized he wouldn't have looked half bad. No, not bad at all. He would have fit right in as a deckhand on his namesake.

Back in her dorm room, Margo lay on the top bunk trying to block out Gina's whimpers from the bottom bed. Maybe sleep gave Gina an escape, too. Thoughts swirled around her mind: Could she really help her father by studying a mental state like alcoholism from Halfway? How could she avoid meeting the Board? And lastly, who were the woman and child in the photo that Thomas held to his heart?

11

1980

MARGO MET REGULARLY WITH six spirits in the Halfway version of Christopher Hayes's science lab. Two handled the equipment setup and material preparation, two managed the execution of experiments, one took responsibility for note-taking, and Margo took charge of oversight—leading the science team to work on new discoveries and cures to cascade down to earth where their findings could change the face of medicine and science.

The lab shift stretched from midnight to sunrise, Newport time. Margo guessed that 12:00 AM coincided with the witching hour. In any event, the tasks at hand called for an adventurous nature.

This morning, Margo proudly passed around copies of her recently completed ten-page alcoholism findings report. "Take a look, guys, " she told the group, "I think it's almost ready to channel to earth."

While her lab partners studied the paper, Margo thought

about all the work behind the document, remembering the night she'd decided to forge ahead with her studies. She had awakened in tears, jolted by the nightmare of her father's slipping helplessly away into alcoholism and depression. At that moment, leaving Gina sleeping in the bunk below her, Margo had gone down into Newport, where she found her father inside the Hawk. Hoping to once again experience the frantic bustle of the kitchen, and the smell of the hamburgers and shrimp grilling to perfection, she instead found the bar closed, her father alone.

She watched Gyp place an empty beer glass under the tap for a refill, then she peered over his shoulder to see the photo album on the bar in front of him. He flipped the pages slowly with one hand, sipping his beer absently, engrossed in the pictures. He ran his fingers over the vivid black and white shots of the two of them fishing off the wharf at the tip of the Narragansett Bay. They'd made a quite a team. She smiled to herself as she remembered the chowder festival contests they won every year. The blue ribbons still hung over the mirrors at the back of the bar.

She longed to reach out and touch his shoulder, to comfort him, but she knew he couldn't see her. As he gazed mutely at each picture, refilling his glass and drinking it down as if he were sleepwalking, she felt tears forming in the corners of her eyes. After a while he laid his head down on the bar's sticky surface and passed out, his cheek cradled by the open scrapbook.

Margo's perky lab partner, Sue, nudged her arm, shaking her from the trance back into the present.

"What about this paragraph?" Sue pointed to a highlighted section in the middle of the page.

Margo addressed the students. "The highlighted paragraph deals with the connection between the loss of a loved one and substance abuse. The pain—and the struggle to numb it—becomes a catalyst for drinking. I'm proposing that there's a physiological or neurological component that needs to be reconsidered."

Margo swung around in a circle on her lab stool, while her peers chattered over the neurological implications of what she'd proposed in the paper. She listened and thought of the one word that could describe her daily life over the past two years: 'obsession.' Researching alcoholism had become her sole compulsion. The more she researched the topic and shared her thoughts with the group in the Halfway lab, the more clearly she saw the growing evidence that alcoholism had a systemic medical root cause, contrary to the current theory that it reflected an emotional handicap—a crutch for the weak.

"You know you can't channel your paper to earth from Halfway, right?" Sue mentioned tentatively.

"Why not?" Margo asked.

"Only the Light can transmit world-changing information. Halfway doesn't allow it."

"Why not?"

Sue shrugged. "Physics, Margo. Or metaphysics, I guess. This is the way the universe works. Maybe because Halfway is only a pit stop and we're still too engaged with the physical."

Margo pondered the other spirit's words. There had to be another way to send her research results to Earth. She would just have to figure it out.

* * *

The sun rose over Providence, flooding the Christopher Hayes campus with light. Margo stood outside the gym, lingering. She knew Gina was waiting for her in Halfway, her hopes set on a 'visitor's pass' to the Light, but she had plenty of time. CHP students strolled by her unhurriedly. Of course, none of them could see her.

She hoped to spy Eddie coming in or going out. Instead, a group of sweaty soccer players passed her and entered the front doors. It didn't matter. If Eddie wasn't at the gym, he probably still lingered in his dorm, hunting for clean shorts. She imagined that, even though the last time she had seen him he had just heard the news that he couldn't play again, he would have defied the odds and been back on the road to the Pros.

She might have simply thought herself there, but instead she walked down the concrete path and into the cafeteria. The smell of eggs and bacon wafted through the room. Students had begun to filter out, lifting their trays of empty plates and milk cartons, dumping their garbage on the corner table. Margo scanned the students' faces as they passed through her and filed out the door. No Eddie, not even a familiar face.

Minutes before first period, Margo grew worried that Eddie would be late for class. Following the remaining students outside, she picked up the pace, jogging through upper campus, and running to lower campus toward Eddie's dorm. In the end, impatient with this human mode of travel, she thought herself to Eddie's room.

Finally, standing just inside the door, looking down on the lanky body buried under the covers, Margo felt a wave of relief wash over her. She tiptoed across the small room to the bed and willed the brown flannel blanket to slip aside so she could see Eddie's face.

Nothing happened.

Positioned over the shapeless lump, she prayed for Eddie to

wake up and come out from under the covers. She thought her prayers had been answered when she heard a cough and the lump stirred. Slowly, a thatch of carroty red hair appeared and the boy sat up and stretched.

"You're not Eddie!" Margo cried.

Her eyes darted across the room, looking for signs of his belongings: his basketball, his gym bag, anything. Instead, she saw a guitar, sheet music, and a basket of books on Shakespeare.

"Eddie, where are you?" She howled, long loud cries that no one—not even this boy who stretched and yawned in Eddie's bed—could hear.

When she joined Gina in Halfway at the track, the visitor pass ceremony had ended, and the three runners from Francis Hall had gone over. Gina remained alone in the stands.

"Sorry I missed them," Margo murmured as she sat down beside her friend.

Gina responded almost inaudibly, smoothing her sundress over her legs. "Whatever."

Margo swallowed hard, fighting her rising fear. "I just visited Eddie's room. His stuff is gone. Where do you think he is?"

"Are you kidding me? You stood me up—*again*—and that's all you have to say!?" Gina exclaimed, incredulously, tilting her head to look at Margo. Her hair looked long, sleek, and glossy black now; her skin, smooth and flawless … because she wanted it that way.

"You promised you would be here early so we could have a moment alone with the soul cleansing board," Gina continued. "Now we will have to wait for another opportunity."

"Did you hear what I said? I looked for Eddie all over CHP. He's not there!"

Gina grasped Margo's shoulder and leaned over to look her

in the eye. "Of course he's not there, Margo. For God's sake, it's *1980*; Eddie graduated two years ago! He's in college now."

Thomas appeared at Gina's side, regarding Margo grimly. "Could you act any less enthusiastic? I mean, at least *pretend* you're a little excited for the runners."

"What for?"

"Gina might get the impression that you have absolutely no interest in a pass. Hell, Gina can't even get you to keep your meetings with the soul cleansing board." Thomas threw up his hands.

"I haven't given it much thought. I don't think Gina cares much what I think about a pass." Margo glanced at Gina, who looked away and shrugged.

"Oh, but she does," Thomas replied tersely. "Have you forgotten what I told you about how passes are given out? They're awarded to a spiritually bound unit. Gina can't get one unless you both ask. You two are bound."

"I forgot."

"Like Hell," Thomas replied. "The ghost that plays by the rules, doesn't easily forget the rules. I'm not buying that line, and I bet neither is your best friend."

Margo didn't want to think about rules. Not now, because she was plotting to circumvent the rule that ideas born in Halfway could only be funneled to the earthly plane from the Light. Yes, she could take her ideas up to the Light by being awarded a visitor's pass, but the thought of going to the Light disturbed her—even frightened her.

She suspected, though, that no rule stated that the idea's author had to be the messenger. She didn't ask, because she didn't want a definite answer. In some cases, better not to know what the universe dictated you couldn't do. Better to beg forgiveness than ask permission.

She turned to Thomas and requested, "Take me to Newport."

"I've invited you to join me on my nightly visits to Newport, but you've always declined. Finally, you agree … while we're discussing your least favorite subject. Awfully suspicious, don't you think? You must be pretty desperate."

Margo avoided his stare. She didn't want to admit that Thomas was right, nor could she explain why he always judged her correctly. She'd actually arrived at the track before the runners had gone over to the Light. She'd seen the envy in Gina's eyes as she hugged them and congratulated them. It had been almost too much to bear.

Almost.

* * *

The *Thomas Tew* nestled in its slip in Newport Harbor. Thomas escorted Margo onto the deck in a quaint act of gallantry. The bar was well stocked with rum, wine and beer. Big, comfortable-looking cushions lined the seats. Margo studied Thomas, his powerful arms rippling with grace as he started the engine and maneuvered the boat past the others and into the empty harbor and spray through the choppy waves. She sat down on the bench behind him.

"Aren't you violating all sorts of metaphysical laws right now?" she asked. "You're touching things."

"What time do you think it is?" Thomas asked in return.

"I don't know. Judging by the fading light, it's around seven PM?"

"It's four AM. That's not fading light, it's the beginnings of dawn. In the same way you have access to earthly knowledge beginning from midnight to sunrise, I can interact with worldly goods during those same hours. Didn't you notice it's pitch black and there's nobody else on the harbor, just you and me?"

"I didn't realize the time," Margo trailed off.

"The longer you're away from the world, the more the whole concept of time becomes … disorienting. That's why when you looked for Eddie on campus this morning, you didn't realize it was 1980. It's not like you're marking off calendars or setting alarm clocks, you only vaguely sense that time is passing."

"How did you know I looked for Eddie?" Margo asked warily.

"I've been shadowing you because the soul cleansing board expressed concern about you."

"Is that the truth?"

"Yes and no. Yes, the Board is worried about you, but no, that's not the only reason I followed you."

"What was the other reason?"

"I felt troubled, too. Time disorientation screws you up. Trust me, I know. And…"

"And what?" Margo demanded.

"And you're still wearing that nightgown."

They'd reached the center of the harbor. Thomas turned off the engine and let the boat drift. Then he stripped down to his trunks and a white t-shirt and dove over the side of the boat. He did not disturb the water. Not a ripple.

Margo leaned over the side of the boat, watching and waiting for him to surface. When he did, he reached up, grabbed her wrists and pulled her over and into the water as if he were a teenaged boy playing in someone's backyard pool. She hit the surface with a splash, spraying salt water everywhere, then surfaced, sputtering, and laughing. She knew he understood the freedom of the open water and the peace that Margo felt being in the harbor. Maybe his love of the sea explained why he'd stayed here for so many hundreds of years.

"I wasn't expecting to go swimming in my nightgown," Margo protested.

"Then take it off," he suggested treading water in front of her. "Or change it into a bright red bikini, or a wet suit, or whatever you like."

His face came so close she could see his white teeth flash in the moonlight. Curiosity filled her; was he *flirting*? She admitted a fleeting attraction to Thomas, but even now, her thoughts turned to Eddie and she knew from the arch expression on Thomas's face that he could read her mind.

She swam away from him toward the boat's ladder then climbed onboard. Thomas followed right behind her. He wrapped a towel around her waist and whispered in her ear, "I'll take you to him."

At the speed of thought, they stood outside the bedroom window of a small clapboard house. Margo's nightgown clung damply to her skin.

"Look inside," Thomas directed quietly.

Margo pressed her face to the window. There Eddie slept soundly, his soft curls framing his face, his bare chest rising and falling with each breath.

"Why did you bring me to the outside of the house? I want to be inside, next to him, I want to hear him breathing. Hear his heart beat. This isn't fair, making me stand out here." She kicked the side of the house with one bare foot, with no sense of pain.

She felt Thomas flinch, even as Eddie shifted and opened his eyes. Had he heard her? Did he feel her presence? She watched as he shook himself awake and threw the covers to one side. He climbed out of bed and came over to the window, opening it.

I can almost touch him.

Margo turned to Thomas. "Are you trying to torture me?"

"Just trying to give you a dose of reality, darling girl. Maybe this is harsh—but life can be harsh sometimes. As you well know."

Margo turned her gaze back to the man in the window, looked into his blue eyes. He was still so beautiful. *When will I ever admit how I feel—how I felt about him*, she wondered.

A door opened, spilling light into the room for a moment before darkness returned. Amy emerged from the bathroom in nothing but a pair of bikini panties and a camisole. Her long hair hung down to her waist. She put her arm around Eddie.

"Come back to bed," she invited.

"Can't sleep," Eddie replied. He covered her hand with his.

She turned to face him, pressing against his side and looking up into his face. "Eddie, why don't we just get married? The house is plenty big to fit me in if you want me. I don't take up much space, you know … a drawer here and there … I'm not greedy." She smiled and kissed Eddie's ear.

He smiled down into her eyes. "You're right," he agreed, while Margo protested that she was wrong, wrong, *wrong*. "We deserve to be a family … and I do love you. Shall I get down on one knee?"

Margo's own knees felt weak. What had happened? How could Eddie marry Amy just like that? It had only been—what—three years? How could he forget Margo when thoughts of him still consumed her?

Margo began to cry. She stretched her arms out toward the open window until only inches separated her from Amy and Eddie. Such magnified senses now. She could see things invisible to the human eye.

Now it's clear.

"Sense anything special?" Thomas asked.

"You know I do." *There are three heartbeats here, not two.*

"Even in death there is life," Thomas murmured.

She grew dizzy as she imagined their future. Eddie would meet Amy at the altar in the family church with only their families as witnesses, then they would settle into their new life in their quaint off-campus cottage where he could be close to his coaching job at CHP.

Margo banged the window with all her might. "It wasn't supposed to be like this!" She crumpled to the grass as if she'd been felled by a sledgehammer.

"So, Red, is this more enjoyable than a swim in the harbor?" Thomas asked wryly. "But stubborn Margo must always get her way. So here we are. Are you having a good time?"

"I just thought I might be mistaken," Margo murmured. "I thought that maybe I was confused that they were together— you know, disoriented, like you explained." She pulled her knees up to her chin and rocked back and forth.

"And with death comes denial," Thomas declared. An awkward pause ensued. "I'm leaving tomorrow."

"Where are you going?" Margo asked. "Are you … crossing over?"

The whole universe seemed to betray her, just like that night in Francis Hall. Her last sight had been fire licking up the dorm room door; her last feeling, a sense of abandonment.

"Madagascar," Thomas replied.

"What?"

"Where I'm going. To Madagascar."

"Why?"

"I need to look for something," he explained.

"Something or *someone*?" Margo stood, smoothing her hair back from her face. "Does it have anything to do with the woman and child in the photo on your mantelpiece?"

He turned away from her. "I'll be gone for a while. I need you to do the night rounds. Check in on the others. Make sure things are going well."

"You mean I'm in charge?" Margo gasped.

He chuckled. "Don't get ahead of yourself."

For one moment, Margo imagined herself in charge of everything. She'd show him. She would be the best-trained, best-informed spirit guide on the entire Francis Hall island. She might make him proud.

She looked up at him. "Will you be disappointed in me if I don't succeed?"

"Oh, you'll succeed," Thomas told her. "You already know this about yourself—you are the exception, not the rule."

12

1990

THOUGH DAYLIGHT HAD ARRIVED, Gina knew that the current residents of room 405 in Francis Hall would still be asleep. Sleeping habits hadn't changed in the last thirteen years of Gina's regular visits to the dorm. The only things that had changed were the students themselves. Sometimes she stuck around to watch them wake up and roll out of bed, marveling at the sloppiness of their baggy pants and ratty collegiate sweatshirts. They barely paused to brush their hair or teeth. Gina wondered how the teachers felt lecturing to a room full of slobs.

Feeling unsettled this morning, Gina stood in front of the full-length mirror hanging on the back of the closet door in the dorm room. She wore a red silk nightgown that highlighted her curvy figure, the same one from the night of the fire. Closing her eyes, she imagined what she'd wear to Carlos's debut art exhibit. When she opened them, she sported a white silk jumpsuit and red pumps. Her long black mane was secured in a high bun on the crown of her head. She wished Carlos could see her. The thought was dumb, but she knew she looked fantastic.

Blowing a kiss to the three sleeping students, she whispered, "I'll be back."

Inside the crowded Providence art gallery, local patrons, RIT students and faculty milled around. In one corner of the room, a group of people queued up at a table where someone was apparently autographing prints and programs. As the line shifted, she recognized Carlos. A news crew hovering at one end of the table surprised her.

"We're from the *Providence Journal*, Mr. Delgado," interjected a male reporter. "Could you break away from your admirers to give us a statement? How do you feel about your paintings getting commercial recognition?"

Carlos stood, leaning on a cane, and detached himself from the cluster of groupies. He awkwardly maneuvered himself over to the reporter and smiled ruefully. "Bittersweet."

"Look this way, please, Mr. Delgado," the *Journal's* still photographer asked politely. "Can you give your fans a grand smile?"

Gina had last seen Carlos a few months ago when she had come to his studio to watch him work. Now, she felt out of touch, as if she'd been away for years. Carlos looked older. And tired. How had he hurt his leg? Had he fallen? She stood next to the photographer and studied Carlos through the lens. His black wavy hair had gone silver at the temples. He wore a white button-down shirt and shapeless blue jeans. He seemed unsteady with the cane, and unaccustomed to using it.

For so long she had been repeating the same actions over and over, hoping for a different result: the earthly studio visits, the apartment hauntings, shadowing Carlos to precipitate a reunion. But nothing ever changed. He lived here and she existed there.

She'd stopped visiting him for a while, but absence only made that feeling of exclusion, of not knowing what was happening in his life, worse than ever.

The gallery curator sidled up to Carlos and whispered into his ear, "I'd like to make a toast to your finest accomplishment. Please ... follow me."

He led Carlos to the front of the room, to a large canvas propped on an easel, then addressed Carlos and the gallery guests, "We know sometimes inspiration comes out of great sorrow. That is the case with this magnificent portrait. Tell us about this painting, *She Haunts*."

Carlos stepped forward and turned the painting into the light. It portrayed a young woman in a red silk dress and a single, long strand of pearls. Gina felt as if she were rooted to the spot.

"The young woman in the painting was the late Gina Manno. This tour de force started as a simple nude sketch of a spunky Italian-American teenager drawn by a very young and very love-sick art student. Her parents ... her family didn't approve of our relationship. When Gina's brother saw the nude sketch and told their father, they felt I had dishonored her. They were ashamed."

The crowd murmured and Gina felt hot tears pricking her eyes.

"I acted like a careless, arrogant kid," Carlos explained. "And for that I am sorry. I hope *She Haunts* will honor Gina's memory."

"Cheers, Carlos."

Gina turned in the direction of the familiar male voice and saw her older brother, Sal, standing in the middle of the pack of guests, his champagne class held high.

Carlos bowed. "Thank you. Now, I'd like to raise a toast to Gina." He turned toward the portrait and lifted his glass. "Your face in the portrait mirrors the expression on your visage the last day I set eyes on you. I will always believe you came to me the day after you … after you passed. I saw you in the corner of my studio, and I appreciated the chance to look upon you one last time. If you're here with me today … I'll be in touch." He smiled and sipped his champagne.

The crowd burst into applause.

I'll be in touch. If only Carlos knew how Gina, too, desired to be in touch—to touch him every day. If he'd seen her once, maybe he could see her again.

Caught up in the joyous mood, she floated toward Carlos, inserting herself between him and the curator. She wanted to stroke his face, but knew better, so she busied herself trying to see what Carlos had done to his leg. She knelt down and reached for the bottom of his blue jean hem. What she felt beneath wasn't flesh and blood; his leg had been amputated.

She took a quick, sobbing breath and backed away. Her first impulse was to console him, but she couldn't risk the revocation of visiting rights. But she must know what misery transpired during her long absence.

In a blink, she transported to Carlos's apartment. Rampaging through the kitchen, the dining room, and his small study, her extended senses reached to places mortal sight could not. Finally, she entered the bathroom, but even here, there were no clues as to what had happened. Nothing.

Gina felt a pulse of pain ripple through her temples and raised a hand to her head. Her ghost migraine, absent for ages, had reappeared. Thomas had explained hallucinations and disorientation were common for spirits, and to be prepared if and when they happened. She pushed through her panic only to feel the pain intensify.

Not real, she told herself. But it didn't help. She turned to the familiar habit from her lifetime. She drew bath water, slipped out of her jumpsuit, and stepped into the tub. Reaching for a washcloth, leaning back, and folding it over her eyes, she prayed for the pain in her temples to subside. She allowed herself to feel the heat of the water—*made* herself feel it.

The pain only deepened. Desperate for any measure of relief, she rose from the tub and wrapped a thick white towel around her body, tucking the ends into the top above her chest. She opened the medicine cabinet that revealed prescription bottles of varying sizes lining the three shelves. Gina understood taking mortals' medicine violated the rules, and was probably futile, but her raw nerves and the unbearable throbbing dictated her movements.

She grabbed the largest bottle and scanned the label. The medication treated osteogenic sarcoma. Carlos had bone cancer. She let the bottle fall from her hand, the large, shiny, black pills spilling onto the tile floor.

"I'll be in touch." Carlos had stated before at the gallery; now she understood.

* * *

Eddie sat back in his chair, lit a cigarette, and clenched it between his teeth. Although the other members of his support group were all of bunch of cry babies, this beat the alternative of jail, where he would have landed last Saturday night had it not been for his father. The perks of being the son of an Irish cop in Boston. He folded his arms across his chest and slumped down in his chair.

The school administration had dropped the assault charges as long as he agreed to address what faculty called his "anger management" problem. He had been drunk the night of the incident, so the school also demanded he attend Alcoholics Anonymous meetings. He laughed remembering how he'd broken the ref's jaw—a clean, sweeping punch, one shot. He should've expected trouble because he'd had a few beers before arriving at his first basketball game as head coach. During the second half, the ref had gotten under his skin by ignoring blatant fouls against his players. Eddie had challenged the official and received a verbal warning. He'd responded with a right hook.

Tonight, the counselor—a slender woman in her early 60s, addressed the recent publication of a groundbreaking paper in *AMA Journal* about the link between physical depression and alcoholism.

"The article," she described, "covers the connection between alcoholism and grief. According to the authors, the same sort of loss that triggers depression, may also cause physiological changes in the brain that incline a person to abuse alcohol."

Eddie thought about Margo's father, and was heartened to know about the growing body of evidence describing alcoholism as a disease and not a character flaw. His mind wandered from the topic as he flicked his ashes into a Styrofoam cup.

* * *

Margo studied Eddie from a corner of the room. In the last couple of years, death had been academically rewarding, but her satisfaction soared this year because a group of living scientists hand-picked by Margo and her team had published her paper on the genetic and neurological roots of alcoholism. At last she had contributed to the medical field. Maybe, just maybe, if she persisted in making scientific advances for the world, she might escape the fate she increasingly felt certain she deserved.

She continued to meet with her science group weekly. They had researched and written many papers that the Francis Hall runners successfully channeled to Earth. The papers should have been delivered to the physical plane only by the author, not via a third party. But Margo was in charge of their region of Halfway—at least as long as Thomas remained in Madagascar.

After watching Eddie for a while, Margo moved to where she could stare into his eyes. She brushed the very tips of his curls with her fingertips. It had always been an utter pleasure to be around him, even at the lowest points of their relationship. But coupled with that pleasure was torment. This new feeling didn't surprise Margo. She took the torment for what it represented: irrefutable proof of her fate.

Margo became conscious of another presence—a spectral presence. Without breaking Eddie's gaze, she commented, "You're back."

"Only for a few hours," Thomas replied.

Margo turned to look at him. He wore a black peacoat with sliver buttons down the front.

Margo pecked his cheek. "How long have you been gone?"

"Ten years. I see we're still having trouble with time orientation." He stuffed his hands in his pockets. "And with progressing to the next stage of your existence. Something tells me you haven't done much toward crossing over while I've been gone. I take it still no visitor's pass with Gina?"

"I don't care about making progress for a pass. Look what

I've done on the subject of alcoholism. This group is reading about my research now. "

"Yes, I heard you're a medical success in the Halfway. You did it, only I don't know how you got your papers to Earth, since you and I both know the papers need to be channeled to earth from the Light and since you don't have a visitor's pass..."

Margo cut him off. "If you're only back a few hours, what are you doing here at a Boston AA meeting?"

"Come to Madagascar with me."

"Are you crazy?"

"I only have a little more time to spend there. Who knows, a change of scenery might do you good."

"But I love it here, in New England, that is, " she replied vaguely. "Why would I want to leave?"

"You mean why would you want to leave *him*?" He tilted his head toward Eddie. Then he simply disappeared.

13

THE SOUTH SIDE BOSTON high school gymnasium sizzled with excitement. The varsity basketball game extended into overtime with seven seconds left on the clock. Eddie stood in front of the bench before his players, dressed in a wool blazer and khakis, radiating confidence.

The crowd roared as the starting five jogged to the middle of the court when the time-out ended. Hanging off to the side with her back to the audience gave her time to think about what had been nagging her since her last Eddie sighting. She didn't remember seeing a wedding ring on his finger.

Now, sitting only a few feet away from him, she tried to catch a glimpse of his left hand, but he kept jumping up to move up and down the court, yelling to the players and motioning plays. Finally, when he called another time out, she drew close to him and grabbed his hand, pulling it toward her, not caring how many rules she broke. She did care that she'd spooked him.

He shook his arm free and yelled at the player next to him, "What?"

When the kid just blinked at him blankly, he pointed to his

clipboard and ordered, "Don, cover Joe for the two-one play and free him up. Run the play just as we practiced it. And all of you: *no fouls.*"

"Expecting a proposal? I mean, now that lover boy is single again."

Thomas materialized next to her, hatless and wearing a tweed waistcoat and striped britches. He looked out of place among the cheering students and parents. "So, I'm right? Eddie is now free from Amy?"

Margo wished he would vaporize. She wanted to relish this moment in solitude, not listen to Thomas's sarcasm, but he was clearly back in her lifeless life.

"Why are you here?"

"I might ask you the same question."

"I don't know what you mean," Margo responded.

"I heard you missed the cheerleaders' Cross-over ceremony. First you missed the runners, now the cheerleaders?"

She shrugged her shoulders. "It's a big day for me. Eddie is single." Margo floated up into a pirouette.

Thomas stopped her in mid-twirl and pulled her back down to earth. "Enough is enough, my darling girl."

"I'm not your darling girl. Let me go. I can take care of myself."

"Not when it comes to Eddie."

"You're being cruel!" Margo complained.

"And you're endangering yourself," Thomas warned.

"I'm dead. What other danger is there?"

"You're in danger of being the hold-out ghost. You and Gina are bound together. She cannot cross over without you. Margo, I'm worried for you. The runners and the cheerleaders have moved on. This leaves Anya, who's up next. She'll have no problems. You know very well that Gina wants to cross, yet you're holding her back. Why?"

"Nonsense. Gina is flourishing in Halfway. There is nothing in the Light for her."

Hearing the game buzzer ring, she turned toward center court. "They won! I need to be closer."

Thomas pulled her back and shook her. "Listen up. Carlos is ill. Very ill."

"More nonsense! Gina hasn't mentioned a word of this to me."

"You're so caught up with your medical research and shadowing Eddie, you probably wouldn't have heard even if she had told you." Thomas held her by both shoulders. "Listen, I'm back from Madagascar for good. You're no longer required to be in charge."

"I didn't mind."

"I didn't think you would. Come with me." He grabbed her arm.

She tried to shake free. "Let me go."

"Not this time."

She stood in a living room in front of a blazing fireplace. She turned to see Thomas lounging casually on a love seat pouring a little tip of red wine into a crystal glass. "Since when do you drink wine?" Margo asked.

"I couldn't find any rum in the cabinets. Hell, when I lived here there was rum in abundance—cases of it, stored all over the house."

"This is your house?"

"Yes, we're in Newport," Thomas confirmed. "The current owners are sound asleep upstairs. May I?" He handed her a glass of merlot.

"What would be the point?" Margo turned to look at the

room, admiring the decor—antiques neatly arranged, oil paintings of highly decorated men dressed in nineteenth century clothes, impressive antlers over the arched hall entrance, large windows facing east and west.

Thomas pulled a pipe from his waistcoat, lit it without a match, and inhaled. "This mansion sits behind a great wall of stone on Newport's finest street. Built in 1640, the original architecture, stone walls, wood paneled rooms, Persian rugs ... are all still intact. The only thing that's changed is the owners."

"Do you visit often?" Margo asked as she sat down cross-legged in front of the fireplace.

"I last came when I was alive, the morning I left for Madagascar the final time."

"Tell me about it."

He tossed back the rest of his wine. "Lydia, my wife, begged me not to go. I think she had a premonition."

"Is she the woman in the photo?" Margo got up and moved to join him on the sofa.

Thomas nodded gravely and raised his glass. "We had a daughter, Pearl."

"The young girl in the photo. I remember."

Thomas reached over and patted her knee. "I was the wealthiest privateer in Rhode Island, and somewhat of a celebrity. I had turned pirate, by then, and successfully taken over an Indian mogul's ship loaded with jewels. Had pounds of gold buried in the garden. Some of it's still there. But I was greedy. I wanted more. So when asked to lead a crew to Madagascar to take over another mogul prize, I said yes. I told Lydia that this would be my last run. Then I would take it easy and spend more time with her and Pearl."

"The thrill of it all must've been difficult to resist," Margo guessed.

Thomas had managed to finish two bottles of wine; just watching, Margo felt drunk. Why did he do this, she wondered? Why did he put on a show of still being ... alive?

The combination of warm fire and Thomas's soothing voice made Margo feel drowsy. His words poured over her like a soft blanket. She settled back into the couch.

Thomas nodded. "Yes, to someone like you or me. That's why you're different from Lydia. She thought anything was enough, you think nothing is never enough." He gave her a crooked smile

Thomas understood her, Margo thought, lifting her bare feet to the coffee table. "So, you went to India for your final pirate run?"

"Yes. I never made it back."

"What happened?"

"In 1694, my vessel was a seventy-ton sloop named the *Amity*. She carried eight guns and a crew of forty-six officers and men. We stopped in Madagascar for a few months. I guess it's what you'd call a pit stop. I had spent almost a year there during my prior voyage. In September 1695, a twenty-five-ship mogul convoy slipped past the island headed north toward the Gulf of Aden. We noticed that the slowest ship in the flotilla lagged quite a bit behind the others, over-laden with goods. The prize tempted us too much to ignore. I took the *Amity* in pursuit. We overtook the ship—the *Fateh Muhammad*—in the Mandab Strait, right at the mouth of the Red Sea, and attacked. I was killed in that battle."

"The hole in your stomach," Margo surmised.

He opened the top buttons of his shirt and kicked off his boots. "Took a cannon ball. Ripped right through my guts. I stood there holding them in my hands in front of the entire crew. A bloody mess."

Margo could see the ragged edges of the open wound above the pristine white of his shirt. "Tragic and swift deaths for both of us. I have no physical reminders, not even a scratch."

"Your scars, my dear Margo, are all inside," he pointed to her temple.

"You mentioned you spent a year, then a few months in Madagascar. What happened in Madagascar that keeps you visiting after over three hundred years?"

He chuckled. "Inquisitive tonight, aren't you? One of the crew members of the *Amity* told me I had a son in Madagascar. I hoped to return to there to see if there was any truth to it. I never got the chance. But in my gut, what's left of it anyway, I know it's true."

"Is your son in the Light? Or is he in Halfway?"

"Never came to Halfway. I'm assuming he too became a pirate or some other kind of murderous thief. Maybe he went straight to Hell."

"Why do you think that?"

"Because that's the only destiny a bastard son of mine could have," he sighed with resignation.

"Don't you wonder what he might have been like? Maybe you're wrong and he became a doctor or a lawyer or a merchant."

He laughed. "Trying to butter me up?"

"Why don't you cross over? Then you could at least be with Lydia and Pearl."

He rocked forward and slammed his wine glass down on the coffee table, sending glittering shards of glass into the ether. "Didn't you hear what I said? There's no crossing over into the Light for me. I would go right into Darkness."

Margo started to pick up the largest pieces of glass, but Thomas stopped her.

"Those are in our dimension, not the land of the living." A second later, the glass disappeared.

Margo looked up at Thomas, but he'd turned so that she couldn't see his face. "So instead you just roam Newport hoping to bump into Lydia?" she asked gently.

"The disorientation on my earthly visits used to make me think I saw her on a boat, at a restaurant, on moonlit walks," he reminisced, still not looking at Margo. "I would cry for her, yell for her, but she never responded."

Margo remembered Eddie's reaction to her trying to hold his hand. "Why? Couldn't she hear you?"

Finally, he turned to look at her. His eyes were full of anger. "It wasn't Lydia. It was you. I mistook you for her time after time. You're not the only spirit who gets trapped inside the maze of disorientation."

"Wait," Margo remembered. "That was you that night in Eddie's room then again at the lighthouse ... when I was ... when Eddie and I...?"

Thomas sighed and reached up to brush her cheek. "You look so much like Lydia, your eyes, your small nose, even your hair, though she wore hers in a bun, not free the way you do." He moved his hand to the loose curls that hung in her eyes.

"I heard distant cries and I ... well, you know. To this day I wondered who it was."

The fire popped and cracked and Margo imagined the heat warmed her body. She fingered the neckline of her cotton nightgown.

"I always searched for Lydia and found you—always you." He

touched her cheek. "In a way, I think I'm almost as much in love with you as I am with Lydia."

Margo looked down, opened her mouth to speak.

Thomas put his index finger to her lips. "Don't say a word. I've always known that you're in love with someone who's still living. I meant to protect you from yourself when I ought to have protected you from me. I've lost Lydia as you've lost Eddie. Perhaps now, we have only each other."

Margo fixed her eyes on him, then reached up to stroke his hair. His face glowed in the firelight. It was a pleasant face, Margo thought. A face that believed in her, trusted her, and loved her.

Thomas took her hands in his and their fingers interlaced. His touch felt good. He leaned in and found her mouth, kissing her hard, almost violently. She seemed to die all over again, feeling the loss of Eddie's touch, his kiss, his strength. But Thomas was right: Eddie and Lydia weren't here, Thomas was, and he wasn't stopping at her mouth.

Thomas pushed her gently back against the couch cushions, and lifted her nightgown off over her head. It was the first time she'd had it off since … since she'd died in it. He made his own clothes simply vanish; his cannon ball wound with them. She permitted him to caress her as if he were clinging to something he could not let go. She reciprocated, reaching for his shoulders, pulling him down encouraging him to explore her Halfway body, a little shocked at the way she kissed him back with such force. He buried her in kisses and embraces, and she, suddenly wild, wanted more. She succumbed to the 15th century pirate — the arrogant leader, ruthless murderer, loving family man, and equally lost soul.

As the sun rose and their 'witching hour' ended, Margo

watched as Thomas postured in front of the fireplace, fully clothed in a white linen shirt with puffed sleeves, a crimson waistcoat with a satin sash, wool trousers and a tricorn hat made of felt and leather.

"What's the occasion?" Margo asked. "I thought hats made you itch."

"Carlos's wake is about to start. He died yesterday."

Riding a wave of guilt, Margo stood up and reached for her nightgown. "Gina will need us."

"Don't you think it's time for you to expand your wardrobe?"

"What do you mean?"

"Do you really still need that nightgown, Margo?"

"Need it? I—"

"How often have I told you that Halfway is what you make of it? You choose to hang onto the trappings of your death. Maybe it's time for a change."

"How?"

Thomas gave her a look. "You know how."

Out of nowhere, Thomas produced a short-sleeved navy blue dress with white piping running along the bottom. "Don't worry, you can still go bare foot."

Margo slid the dress on and combed her hair with her fingers.

"This will change things you know … Carlos's death," Thomas proclaimed solemnly.

"Everything changes. Did I tell you about the ultrasound discovery the biology team is working on?"

"Don't change the subject. Gina is going to want to see Carlos and I'm not sure he's coming to Halfway; he's had years to prepare himself for death. At some point you're going to have to face whatever it is you're hiding from."

"I'm not hiding from anyone," Margo claimed.

"I didn't say someone, I said some*thing*. It's not just your attachment to Eddie that's causing you to resist crossing over . Broken hearts heal. If you had spent any time with the Soul Cleansing Board preparing for Cross-over, you would've learned that the hardest spirits to cross over are those filled with guilt and remorse."

"I can't think about that now," Margo noted, pausing to check her reflection in the mirror hanging over the fireplace. She experimentally rearranged her hair with a thought and added a necklace to her wardrobe, then low pumps. "Can't we just talk about the ultrasound? It's going to change the diagnostic industry. The medical field hasn't seen anything like it."

"Well, since you insist on talking about your research, I can't let you continue to give your medical insights to other souls to channel."

"But the ultrasound," Margo gasped. "What about the ultrasound?"

"You, as the source of the research, have to pass the documents to the physical world from the Light yourself. You can no longer send them via a third party like you've been doing. Besides that, you've been relying on the loyalty of those souls— trading on their sense that they owe you something for trying to save them. But that only goes so far. Those souls are only going to put up with visitor's passes for so long before they want to cross over for good. Meanwhile, poor Gina hasn't even been allowed a visit. Because of you, Margo."

Margo felt, for the first time, the full awkwardness and vulnerability of being suspended between Heaven and Earth … and Hell. Thomas was right about remorse. Certain pieces of that night were immediate, blurry, and monstrous. Time passage, for example. Just how much time had passed from the moment she had wakened to a strange smell, to the time she knew she had drawn her last breath? It seemed like an instant.

Other pieces of the night were drawn out and surprisingly vivid. The walls of flame barring them from rescue, the slow dance of the smoke that slithered down the hall like a hungry tiger, intent on its prey. During those moments of clarity she had wracked her brain over and over, trying to determine how it had come to this. She wanted to blame the age of the dormitory and its lack of multiple fire escapes or the hallway decorated with Christmas wrapping paper and hanging lights. She wanted to believe someone had dropped ashes from a cigarette.

She knew better. She owned the mistake —the girl who'd found a clever use for a hairdryer. The fire started in the bathroom with a hairdryer and, she knew, a pair of soggy red mittens. *Her* red mittens.

If she wanted to rescue herself from Hell, she had to accrue enough positives to balance her account, didn't she? All she had to give—all—was her medical breakthroughs. And now it seemed even they were to be taken away.

She thought about Thomas's advice, and about Gina. She had held Gina back; what side of the balance sheet did that fall on?

* * *

Gina paced back and forth in the Providence funeral home's foyer. Her brother Sal entered the front doors. He wore soft brown corduroys and a sweater vest. Taking a long puff on a cigarette, he tamped it out surreptitiously in a planter by the door.

She followed her brother into the private viewing room.

Dark red velvet curtains covered two high windows. The mourners sat in graceful straight-back chairs arranged in five rows of six. A table stood against the rear wall with a visitor's registry, which Sal paused to sing, resting on top. He lowered himself onto the long settee in the back on the opposite side of the door, and stared at the coffin laying atop a bier to the left of the chapel's altar.

Gina found herself standing beside the coffin, not really conscious of how she had gotten there. Within it, Carlos lay peacefully, his skin pale against a lining of red satin.

He's not really in there anymore, she told herself. *It's just a shell.*

Still, she stood next to the shell and observed the ritual: each person in the line of mourners moved to pay their respects to the Delgado family seated in the front row of the chapel, then paused before the altar to light a prayer candle, murmur a few words or simply bow their heads. Some made the sign of the cross.

Sal was last in line. Gina watched him kneel before the altar, saw him make the sign of the cross and mumble a prayer for Carlos's soul. Then he came to the coffin and peered down into it. Reaching into his back pants pocket, he came up with the nude sketch of Gina and tucked it under Carlos's folded hands, next to his heart.

Gina remembered the night Sal had grabbed it so furiously from Carlos during a Sunday night dinner in 1976. A night that, to Gina, seemed like a lifetime ago because it had been.

With the processional over, Gina waited for Carlos to appear. After all, she had attended her own funeral and expected the same of him. But only mortals remained. No spirits. Friends and family stood and spoke about Carlos, and still Gina waited. Carlos still did not come.

Mourners surrounded her. Carlos's family wept, his mother clinging to the rosary, fellow faculty and students hugging each other and whispering of Carlos's virtues, and Providence artists discussing which of Carlos's paintings would bring the most at auction. Still, Carlos did not appear.

Enraged and desperate to call him forth, Gina tore off the red silk dress she had worn in whimsical honor of *She Haunts*, and naked, screamed to the heavens, "I'm here! Where are you? I need you! Forget the damn sketch! Here's the real thing!"

She turned to scan the room in a fit of despair, and found Thomas and Margo on either side of her.

"Looks like we got here just in time," Margo commented. She retrieved the silk dress and handed it to Gina.

Gina threw it aside; it disappeared into the ether. "Why isn't Carlos here? I thought all spirits attended their own funerals."

"Not all, " Thomas explained gently. "Everyone's path into the next life is different."

Gina felt Margo's arm around her shoulders.

"Don't worry, Gina," Margo consoled her. "Carlos will be in Halfway by now, waiting for you. He can join your art group; he can paint you; you can even paint together and roam RIT during your earthly visits."

Gina looked up, "What if you're wrong? What if there's no pit stop for Carlos? He knew death was coming. He had years to prepare. There's no reason for him to stop off in Halfway for preparation. He's not attached to a person place or thing on Earth and he's not harboring any remorse."

She clothed herself again, this time in the red nightgown she'd been wearing in death. It seemed appropriate, somehow, she felt as if she were starting her own journey in Halfway over again. Before she had time to consider what do to next, Anya appeared beside her. She had a piece of sketch pad paper in her hand. Gina recognized it immediately. The sketch Sal had just placed in the coffin.

Anya held out the drawing. "I've just come from the Light to give you this."

Gina put her hands to her face. Beneath her spectral finger-tips, her face felt ridged, leathery, burned. "Oh no,"she moaned. "Dear God, no!"

She had waited all these years, and he had sailed right past her. Believing Carlos might come to Halfway, as slender a hope as it had been toward the end, had kept her from hating Margo for holding them both here.

"Gina, it's all right," Anya reassured her. "Carlos isn't coming to Halfway, but he's waiting for you in the Light. He gave me the sketch as proof."

Gina glanced at the sketch of her nude body—her porcelain skin without any traces of tragedy. "I can't take this anymore!" she cried. "I want to be with Carlos!"

Before she half-thought about it, she had lifted an empty chair and flung it across the room. Mourners looked up, cried out, some backed away.

Margo stepped in front of her. "You're scaring everyone," she warned. "Get hold of yourself."

Gina met Margo's gaze, feeling as if she would burst into flame if she did not speak up for herself now. "Margo," she cried, her voice full of anger and hurt, "you have kept me here long enough. I want a visitor's pass to the light."

PART III

"IT IS NOT THE MOUNTAIN WE
CONQUER, BUT OURSELVES."

— SIR EDMUND HILLARY

14

1995

MARGO STOOD ON THE slippery rocks beneath the Newport lighthouse and watched its light shine into the fog swirling up from the bay in the afternoon sunlight. A small speedboat cut through the choppy waves of the Narragansett Bay. No living person looking in that direction would notice it. She thought it must be the runners and Anya.

"Help me with the blanket," Gina ordered from behind her.

Margo leapt from the rocks to the tufts of grassy sand at the base of the lighthouse and grabbed the edges of the beach blanket, unfolding it onto the ground. Gina set a white bakery box in the center.

"This is nice," Margo commented. "Where's everybody else?"

"Oh, um, they'll be here," Gina promised. She sat down on the blanket and picked at the string tied around the box.

Margo turned back to the water. "I see a boat, but the fog is too thick to make out any of the girls."

"Sit down," Gina commanded. "Look at your cupcakes.

Vanilla with chocolate icing, your favorite." She lifted one from the box and held it out.

"Hey, thanks for organizing a birthday party for me," Margo smiled, barely glancing at the cupcake. She kept her eyes trained on the water, tracing the path of the boat as it came closer.

"It's nothing … really," Gina demurred. "It's not every day a girl turns thirty-one." She patted the blanket. "Come on. Sit down."

"Wait a sec." Margo shaded her eyes with her hands as the boat pulled up to the rocks and a single person got out. She recognized him as one of the members of the soul cleansing board. "I see," Margo bristled. She turned and glared at Gina. "So this is my birthday party?"

Gina jumped to her feet and grabbed Margo's arm as if she were afraid Margo might transport herself away. "Margo, it's been five years since Carlos died. Every time I ask you to make our first Soul Cleansing Board meeting, you make an excuse."

"I've been busy," Margo offered, trying unsuccessfully to pull her arm free.

"Don't I know it," Gina remarked bitterly. "I could recite the excuses in my sleep: your lab work, your CHP visits and your many Newport rendezvous with Thomas. I'm desperate to see Carlos, but I can't get a visitor's pass without you. What else can I do to make you have the meeting?"

"Your friend is here." Margo grimaced as the Board member, a dark-haired man, with an air of solidness to his countenance, approached.

"Hello, Margo. My name is Victor." He folded his hands over his stomach. "The Board thought it best if I came alone for our first meeting."

His gaze traveled from Margo to the lighthouse to the bay. "It's beautiful here. I can see why you feel so safe in this setting."

Gina dropped Margo's arm and confided, "We're both really excited for our Cross-over preparation and visitor's passes."

"Speak for yourself," Margo warned, flopping down onto the blanket.

Gina launched into an obviously well-rehearsed speech, but Victor cut her off with a soft wave of his hand. "I know your position, and understand your eagerness for a visitor's pass. This is not our issue here today." Victor lowered himself lightly onto the blanket. "Margo," he sighed, "management has never been in this predicament. You've really stumped us."

"What do you mean?"

"Well … you've been in Halfway for eighteen years and have yet to meet the SCB."

"Is that so unusual?" Margo asked.

It wasn't as if she hadn't been a contributing member of the Halfway region. She had thrown herself energetically into playing the role of apprentice to Thomas and had succeeded—or at least that's what everyone claimed. She'd been a clever girl now turned into an equally clever ghost. She'd made earthbound compliance decisions when Thomas traveled in Madagascar. She'd pioneered the discovery of the link between disease and alcoholism in the late 70s. Her science group voted her head lab technician. Margo was an absolute wonder; everyone said so.

"Not so unusual, no," Victor agreed. "Heck, Thomas arrived here over one hundred years before we got him to even sit down and talk to us."

"So what's the problem? I'm no different from Thomas."

"But you are, my dear. Thomas, you see, arrived alone. His actions don't impact anybody else."

"I see where you're going with this." Margo picked at some blades of grass poking through the blanket. "Gina and me."

"Exactly. You and Gina cannot even receive a visitor's pass to the Light, because such passes are given in units and the two of you are a unit. Isn't that true?"

Margo didn't answer.

"I know tricking you into this meeting was dishonest," Gina conceded, "but it's for your own good."

"My own good? What do you or anybody else know about my own good?" Margo's voice cracked. "I can't stay here."

"Please listen to what Victor has to say." Gina begged.

Margo cringed at the desperation and pain in her voice. But Gina didn't understand. No one could understand, not even Thomas. Margo stared at the cupcake, then at the beautiful sight of the misty tendrils of fog advancing across the water. This was her favorite earthly spot, the place she had come to when she first left life; but now all she could see were the flames of that night in Francis Hall. All she could hear were the screams. The smell of burning skin overwhelmed the scent of sea breeze.

Escape always eluded her.

"I can't breathe," she gasped, struggling to her feet.

Gina threw her arms around Margo and held her. "Stop going back to that place, that night. I have my scars; you have your memories. It's time to move on."

"There is no moving on. At least not for me. " She broke from Gina's embrace. "I'm not ready."

Moments later, Margo stood in the center of Christopher Hayes' campus in front of the student union. In the nippy, late afternoon air, students wore heavy sweatshirts and walked past her quickly.

She climbed the steps of the student union, pleasant memories flooding her mind as she entered the building: collecting letters from home, meeting Eddie at the coffee shop, spending inordinate amounts of time in the science lab and library. Inside, the usual chatter filled her ears. Margo stood next to two girls sharing a can of soda and flipping though their mail. Teachers hurried through the area, off to the adjacent faculty room.

Margo's attention was drawn to a student across the room, standing last in line at the coffee shop. She crossed the room and hovered next to him. Dressed in a red flannel shirt and tattered Levis with a single hole in the right knee, his layered light brown hair hiding one side of his face, the boy squinted up at he menu board and rubbed his eyes. They were blue. And lovely, Margo thought. Fate tempted her to trace the contours of his lean cheekbones and long face with her fingertips.

He ordered a large black coffee with two sugars, took the Styrofoam cup from the cashier and sipped at his coffee noisily.

Two other students waved to him from a corner booth, "Over here."

The boy waved back and started toward them.

"Don't go," Margo begged.

He froze. She recognized the queer look, the startled reaction from someone who had just sensed her presence.

He shook his head and strode away. Abruptly, Margo put herself in front of him, blocking his way. He walked right through her. She moved in front of him again. Nothing. When he reached his friends, they gave him a warm salute and slapped him on the back.

She willed him to turn around so she could look into his eyes but he stayed facing his friends. A combination of cold excitement and an odd tenderness came over her. He was easily the most beautiful person in the room … she felt as if she knew him.

After standing motionless for some time, she felt someone with her. "What are you doing here?" she wondered.

"Why did you leave?" Gina asked.

"I'd rather be here. Don't you miss it?"

"Not really," Gina replied with a wry smile.

"But our times together in the dorms? All those nights in the hall with the girls, studying and hanging out?"

"I do miss our dorm and our roomies, but it's not the same. I'll show you."

Inside Francis Hall, Room 405, a girl wrapped in an old cotton robe hunched over a laptop, methodically hitting the keyboard. The girl looked like she'd just woken up even though it was two in the afternoon. Margo and Gina glanced at each other and laughed.

"Sleeping in—I guess that's the same," Gina admitted, grinning.

"So you're right," Margo admitted, as she plopped on the bottom bunk's mussed bedcover. "Electric typewriters have been replaced with computers. That's not that big of a change."

"Look around," Gina urged. "Crock pots are gone," she eyed the microwave on top of the mini fridge.

"I guess I've been spending all my time in the science lab and hadn't noticed the changes to the dorm," Margo remarked. "I remember racing you to the payphone in the hall … that gone too?"

"Yup."

The girl stood up and went to the closet, putting on a trench coat and green rubber boots. She tucked her long blonde hair under a rain hat, grabbed a backpack from the bed, and closed the door behind her as she left.

"She forgot her umbrella," Gina laughed as she rummaged through the closet. "Look, the only dress in the closet." She held a blue silk dress with white piping against her and walked like a model, with an exaggerated swing of her hips. "I love the lace on top, but the skirt is so full and has tulle at the bottom," she twirled in a circle, making the bottom flare. "Even the clothes have changed. I don't see any painter pants, patchwork skirts, or halters."

"I just visited last week," Margo remembered, picking up a biology textbook and leafing through its well-marked pages. "Seems strange."

"You only think you were here last week," Gina replied.

"So what are we doing here now? I was quite happy at the coffee shop."

"Victor suggested I show you the changes that have taken place on campus as a reminder that time is moving on."

"Oh, I see—another setup," Margo complained, her eyes glued to the calendar tacked to the bulletin board: October 1995. "Do you think students even remember the fire here?" she asked soberly.

"Don't know," Gina replied. "That time in history is so far from their everyday lives. There reminders continue, though: surprise fire drills, annual fire department inspections, new fire escapes, new wiring, new rules about dormitory decoration. You can't decorate the halls at Christmas time the way we used to."

"What about hair dryers?" Margo asked.

"Leaving them plugged in is the most dangerous fire hazard, actually. Why do you ask? Planning to blow dry your hair now?"

"No. I just wondered." Margo thought again of that night, of the hairdryer and the mittens, then pushed the thought from her mind.

"I'm going to see him," Gina shared, after a long pause.

"See who?" Margo asked.

"Carlos."

"But how is that possible?"

"After you left the lighthouse, I explained everything to Victor. I told him I'm desperate for a visitor's pass to the Light but I'm stuck because you and I are a unit and you're showing zero intent to transform enough to cross over. In fact, I don't think you'll ever leave Halfway … and where does that leave me? It's not fair and, as it turns out, God is all about justice. So's Victor. I told him I officially give up trying to convince you to change, but he asked me to try a little harder, and in exchange he granted me a special visitor's pass to the light."

"What do you mean by special?" Margo asked.

"The soul cleansing board made an exception about giving out passes in units. And … it's limited. I can go, but I'll be called back sooner than for a normal pass."

"But I thought what about me?"

"This isn't about you. It's about me, and what's fair. They overruled the unit stipulation to be fair to me, because you're not cooperating. So, I get one; you don't." Gina shook her head in disgust. "I just don't get it. You know your medical insights can't travel to Earth from the Light anymore, so what is it? Are you in love with Thomas, now? There must be more you're not telling me."

Margo walked over to the window and looked out at the quad. Gina, the soul cleansing board, Thomas—all had asked her over and over again to show enough progress to cross over, and not once had she given it serious consideration.

"Cant' we change the subject?" she asked. "I want to talk to you about something." Margo told her about the CHP student she'd seen in the coffee shop in the student lounge. "I think he felt me somehow, I don't know how. Do you think that's why I'm drawn to him?"

"Could be. Some people could be more sensitive to us. You know fortune tellers and psychics."

"Do you believe in it?" Margo asked. "In ESP and all that?"

"No."

"Come with me to the student union. Maybe the boy will be there and you can see what I mean," Margo explained.

Gina sighed. "I brought you to our old dorm room to get you over the past, but I guess it isn't working."

"Don't you get it Gina? I'm happy."

"Margo, you haven't been to the Light so you really don't know what happiness is."

Margo looked out the dorm window onto the quad as the boy walked across the yard toward the library. "I have some research to do about a new polarization theory. I need to go to the library."

At 6:00 PM, Margo counted on the library being empty at this hour. Seated at a table as she had often been in life, something made her look up— a chill, a tugging at her soul, a warning. It felt like particles of ice in her non-existent heart. The boy from the student center approached her table.

He walked through the library with his head up, arm-in-arm with a pretty young girl with a sweet smile. Margo hadn't realized before how tall he was. His loose, fine hair swung over his high forehead, framing a face not babyish, but vulnerable and very handsome.

For a moment Margo froze. Students passed by her in small steady streams, giggling and talking in low whispers. She waited until the boy and the girl with him found an empty table, then abruptly moved to stand looking down at them as they pulled books out of backpacks and arranged them on the table. The first book out of the boy's bag was *The History of Western*

Civilization, the same one she used to study from, though she could see it had been revised many times. Still required reading, apparently.

Margo parked on the opposite side of the table and eavesdropped on their conversation. His name was Luke, hers was Meg. Luke, the goalie for the varsity lacrosse team, wanted to study political science in college and lived in Gallagher Hall, third floor.

"Where to after this?" Luke asked. "Dempsey's or my dorm room?"

"Dempsey's has fifty cent fountain drinks tonight," Meg remarked.

"Gotta love Thursdays, but what about my room right now?" Luke inquired.

"Why don't' we save that for after Dempsey's," the girl replied, ducking her head demurely.

Margo shook her head. "Nothing's changed, has it?" she ruminated. "It's still the same old game."

Luke shivered and glanced up. "Who said that?" he asked. He suddenly looked very young and frightened.

"I didn't hear anything," responded Meg.

Just then, the head librarian, an older woman with a bun reminiscent of the Victorian era, rang the closing bell. Luke and the girl returned their books to their backpacks and shared a long kiss in front of Almanacs and dictionaries.

"Let's go to Dempsey's." Luke took Meg's arm and steered her towards the exit.

Margo felt compelled to follow them out. She couldn't resist his magnetic youthfulness and beauty.

Outside, raindrops began to fall in the dark night. Margo shadowed Luke and Meg almost mechanically as they walked hand-in-hand through the lower campus playing fields. When they reached the southern gate leading to the off-campus area still 'legal' for Hayes Prep high-schoolers, the rain cascaded down harder. Laughing and dodging puddles, they jogged up the street to the diner. A crack of thunder broke overhead and the sky opened up with a deluge of water that only escalated the couple's laughter, as they clutched at each other on the slippery pavement.

Margo felt a pull in her chest. What would the rest of her life at CHP have been like if death had not claimed her? How might that night in 1977 been different if Eddie had returned to her during that party, as he'd promised? Would he have explained how he missed their relationship and wanted to reunite? If so, would she, not Amy, have slept in Gallagher Hall that night with Eddie? Instead, she had returned alone to her dorm to prop up a hairdryer to dry her red mittens. Funny, she couldn't even remember doing that. Maybe because she so badly wished she hadn't done it. Maybe the memory, even after death, tried to hide things like that.

Luke and Meg reached the intersection to cross over to Dempsey's. The light turned red and the stream of cars slowed to a stop, their headlights glaring in the rain. Luke grabbed Meg's hand as they sprinted across the street. Luke, his arm up shielding his face from the downpour, didn't see the taxi careening around the corner. Slamming on the brakes, the driver skidded toward the couple.

Luke shoved Meg out of the taxi's path, then turned to run but slipped, falling to his hands and knees, staring into the oncoming headlights. To Margo, the scene unfolded in slow motion; she flew forward, picking Luke up and bowling him over onto the sidewalk. The taxi slid past them and crashed into a light pole a few feet away.

Meg ran to Luke, who had tucked himself into the fetal position, rocking back and forth and crying out in pain. Several good Samaritans rushed over. Two stopped to comfort Luke, another looked into the cab and ran to find a phone.

Margo sat on the wet curb long after the police cars and ambulance had come and gone. She knew the consequences of changing the course of a mortal's destiny—revocation of earthly visitation rights. She began to cry.

15

MARGO FLED BACK TO Halfway, straight to Thomas's cottage. When he opened his door, he seemed surprised to see her. Thomas wore a pair of skin-tight knickers that showed off well-muscled calves; and a white shirt open at the throat. One hand held the neck of a dusty bottle of what looked like centuries-old whiskey. Or perhaps only the ghost of centuries-old whiskey.

Spirit spirits, Margo thought, absently, wondering why, after all his years in Halfway, Thomas still maintained his attachment to wine, food, and ... other worldly pursuits.

As if he heard her thoughts, he remarked, "I was expecting a dinner guest, but I can always send her a message to come later, for dessert. I do fancy a sweet dessert, if you know what I mean." He winked. "And, of course, you do."

She hated this mood of his. "I'll can come back later," she turned to go.

"Don't be silly." Thomas took hold of her arm and pulled her into the room. "I'm a fool, but I always prefer your company.

Especially over a woman only willing to provide me small talk and meaningless sex."

"I guess that's a compliment," Margo conceded.

She studied his face for a moment, noticing for the first time a small scar on the right side of his broad forehead. Crows feet surrounded his deep-set blue eyes nestled in his weather-beaten skin, but Margo recognized the kindness in his countenance as he gazed at her. She hesitated, wondering why he let himself look his death age.

"Just passing by and thought I'd stop in."

"You're a terrible liar, " Thomas accused, airily. "But I'm sure a glass of wine will coax whatever haunting antics you've been up to out into the open."

Margo looked at the small oak table laid for dinner in front of the fire. A bottle of Chardonnay poked out of a silver ice bucket.

"I don't think I can stay for dinner," Margo objected, trying to make her voice sound cheery.

"And why not?" Thomas asked. "We can recreate our night together at my home in Newport. I already planned to sail our favorite waters on a moonlight boat ride. Join me." He poured her a glass of the Chardonnay and passed it over to her.

"Thanks," she replied, and made a show of sipping at the wine. She could taste it if she wanted to. She decided she did. If she were alive, she'd need a drink after what had happened with Luke earlier. Margo relaxed as the alcohol's warmth permeated her.

Thomas smiled and his charm cast a spell on her, as well. She leaned in, kissing him lightly on the cheek.

"You know where my treasure is buried," he laughed. "There is no need to seduce me to get my gold." He flopped down in a chair at the table. "So what's bugging you? Do I have to pry it out of you? You know I used to specialize in the art of torture when necessary." At the expression on her face, he roared with laugher and slapped his knee.

"Nothing's wrong. I'm just not that hungry," Margo explained, looking down.

"You must stay." He poured himself a fresh shot of whiskey from his dusty bottle, then unbuttoned the right sleeve of his starched white shirt and rolled it up, exposing his scarred forearm.

Margo joined him at the table and took another sip of wine. Food had appeared; Thomas ate ravenously. She tried to fork an asparagus stalk, but her hands were shaking.

"You look as though you've seen a ghost," Thomas chuckled. "What's wrong? Did your little campus boyfriend, Luke, cheat on you and kiss another ghost?" He bit into his steak. "I need to change the subject. I saw Gina today. She's been at the art studio for two days waiting for Carlos to appear in her earthly visits."

Margo picked at a soft dinner roll. "But, Carlos can't visit Earth—can he?"

"No," Thomas replied. "You know as well as I that once you cross over, there is no desire for earthly visits. But I can't convince your determined roommate. She helplessly waits for Carlos because she is tired of trying to convince you to cross over so she can be with him all the time, not just during stolen moments while on a visitor's pass to the light."

"I see," Margo mumbled, avoiding Thomas's eyes.

"This doesn't bother you?" His intense gaze suddenly unnerved her.

"What doesn't bother me?" She poured herself another glass of wine.

"Oh, come on," Thomas prodded, his voice taking on a sharp edge. "You're a smart girl, a med student no less. You know exactly what I mean. Doesn't it bother you that you're the hold-out ghost and you block Gina?"

"But Gina's able to visit the Light now."

"And that's supposed to be enough? For all eternity? It's only a visitation. Gina longs to stay there permanently with her soul mate."

"What makes you the expert?"

"I *listen* to her when she tells me things. You tune her out. Pretend she means something else, or that because she was only nineteen when she died, her love for Carlos can't be real and eternal. You know when it's the worst? When she's at the Cross-over ceremonies, wishing she could cross over. You haven't seen that anguish, because you've never been to a Cross-over cere-mony. Hell, you had a near-meeting with Victor and fled for CHP in search of your dear Eddie."

Margo stood. "I don't want to hear any more."

"Gina has all but lost hope of living permanently in the Light because of your unwillingness to face the SCB. Have you even seen Gina lately?"

"It's been a while," Margo admitted.

"Yes, it's been a while, because you've been spending most of your time at Hayes. Haunting, haunting, and more haunt-ing. Meeting with your science group doing research that will never reach Earth because you already know you can no longer channel your findings. Whatever you did before you died must have been blasphemous to make you so guilt-ridden. What was it? Did you talk back to your mother? Cheat on your biology exam? Miss midnight mass? Sleep with the hockey team? What is it you don't want to face?"

Margo moved to the window. The view of the clouds and open sky usually brought her solace, but now the flames appeared. The heat. They were always with her, now. Thomas walked up behind her and rested his hands on her shoulders. She barely felt his touch.

"I don't care what sins you committed when you were alive," he murmured into her ear. "I still have a soft spot for you. Let me show you tonight in Newport out on the Narragansett Bay. Let it be me at the lighthouse making love to you. Not Eddie."

Margo started to say, "I don't know," as she always seemed to do. But she *did* know.

So she simply uttered, "No."

"Get over him," Thomas commanded, his voice hard.

"I'll never get over Eddie," she whispered.

She hadn't meant to say it aloud, but she did. The lines of thinking and speaking had blurred. She felt herself losing control, because she acknowledged, for the first time, the truth of those words. Eddie was more than a high school romance. If Carlos was Gina's soul mate, Eddie was hers.

"I don't believe you," Thomas pressed. "Come with me to Newport. We'll leave this instant."

Margo wrenched herself away from him. "No. I'm not some wench you invented to linger outside your bedroom. I don't need you. I don't want you." She turned to face him. The flames were there, all around her. She felt dizzy from the red heat.

"No, you're not one of my wenches. I would die for you if I weren't already dead." He pulled her into his arms and buried his face in her neck. "Make me believe you'll never be over Eddie," he murmured.

She pushed him away, clutching the collar of her white

nightgown closed. "I can't go to Newport with you tonight, tomorrow, ever again."

Thomas took a step back, his eyes bright as he studied her. "What are you hiding, Margo? I can see it. You haven't looked me in the eyes once since you got here."

She made herself meet his eyes. "I changed a mortal's fate," she whispered. "I can't go to Newport anymore."

Thomas's eyes narrowed for moment, the he turned away from her, pacing back to the center of the room. "Who is it?" he asked. "Luke, your latest obsession?" He walked over to the table, grabbed the empty whiskey bottle and hurled it at the wall. Jagged pieces shattered to the floor. Thomas intentionally stepped onto the glass, blood seeping from his feet. Margo stared at him without moving.

"You don't bleed anymore," Thomas noticed. "But you still feel the heat from the fire. The flames are ever present, aren't they? A fucking dysfunctional pair, the two of us." He shook his head, then glanced down at his feet. The bleeding stopped. "But we're not a pair. You made your choice long ago and now you've interfered with a life to ruin what you have in death. You're right, my darling girl, you can't come to Newport with me. You're finished with earthly visits and I fear you may never conquer the roadblock that keeps you from moving forward to the Light."

"But I still have you here in Halfway," Margo inquired, her voice trembling, "don't I?"

Thomas laughed at her. "You're joking right? Is that what you're going to try to convince yourself of next? I can't help you anymore. You're on your own this time."

"What do you mean this time?" Margo asked.

"You need to say good bye to Luke. When earthly visits are revoked, you get one last trip to say goodbye and get closure. "

"But what about Eddie? Can't I see him one last time?" Margo pleaded.

"Perhaps if you can find him," Thomas replied, cryptically.

Margo felt the universe shake around her. "If I can *find* him? Are you saying you've hidden him from me? Is that why I haven't seen him for so long? And to think I believed I had discovered another side of you—the gentle Thomas Tew, the man that Lydia and Pearl must have loved and treasured as their husband and father. But you're evil, really, aren't you—treating people like they're yours to control?" She threw herself at him with a wild sob, and pummeled his chest with her fists. "You can't control me! I won't let you!"

Thomas wrestled her arms to her sides. "You call it controlling you. I call it caring about you—loving you. Blame me for resorting to heartless measures to make you realize what you're costing yourself. You risked your earthly visits by changing a mortal's destiny. You risked seeing Eddie because you felt compelled to insert yourself in another mortal's life. So go say goodbye to your dear student, because you won't be seeing him again for a very long time. And here's the real news, Margo Tracey. I'm not hiding Eddie from you. You've been hiding him from yourself."

He turned his back and dismissed her with a wave of his hand.

"What does that mean?"

"You're clever," Thomas told her. "Figure it out."

* * *

Margo hurried through the bright bustling corridors of Providence Memorial Hospital. The stench of sickness and death buried beneath a layer of disinfectant seemed to close in on her, making her feel light-headed. She damped down her memories of the hospital's atmosphere and wondered what it would have been like if she had lived to become its first female surgeon. She probably wouldn't have found the smell offensive, but invigorating. She certainly wouldn't have been able to just turn it off at will.

She imagined herself marching down this hall with a sense of purpose, just like all the eager and freshly scrubbed doctors rushing past her this evening. The thought made her smile and she felt a weight lifting from her shoulders. This would have been her home; this would have been the place she belonged. She pictured herself in a doctor's scrubs hurrying to a patient's side.

Padding along quickly in her soft-shod feet, she found Luke's room and slipped into the shadows to one side of the door. In the dimly lit room, Luke reclined in a raised bed, his head propped up by pillows. A shapeless nurse with a short, spiky hairdo stood by his bedside, adjusting his IV.

"How're you doing, Luke?" she asked him.

"My ribs hurt like hell," Luke moaned.

"That's because they're broken," the nurse explained. "You'll feel the effects of the morphine soon. Try to rest. The doctor will be in to see you shortly."

Margo inched closer. The accident had left Luke's fingers scratched and bloodied. A cut marred his left cheek.

"The ambulance drivers believe it's a miracle you're alive," the nurse related. "Do you remember any of it?"

Luke stared down at his fingers. "No."

"Well, you are one lucky kid," the nurse remarked as she left the room.

Red Mittens

Margo sat in the empty chair next to the bed. She studied Luke for a moment, then leaned over and stroked his right cheek. The boy shook his head and adjusted his pillow. Then he turned toward Margo and smiled.

"Hey," he whispered.

Margo froze, sudden chaos in her head.

"Hey, kid," a voice called from behind her.

A rush of recognition coursed through Margo's body. She turned and there was Eddie.

He wore a leather jacket and a pair of jeans. He looked gritty and unshaven. His blonde hair still curled around his forehead, with only a streak or two of grey.

Margo started to tremble. Frozen in the chair, she waited, mesmerized. Eddie moved his hands in and out of his pockets, trying to feign nonchalance, but breathing heavily, as if he had just run a great distance.

"So, uh, what does the other guy look like?" he joked.

The nurse stuck her head in the door. "Oh, it's you, Mr. Sullivan. Your son had a losing battle with a taxi cab."

* * *

The center of the Light of Heaven emanated a pleasant warmth. No crowds marred the pristine beach; a group of spirits played volleyball in the perfect temperature of the Light-filled ether, while others looked on. Gina had been wandering her favorite places, looking for Carlos without finding him. Her visitor's pass allowed her only a finite length of time before she must return to Halfway. Her internal clock set the subjective time at about thirty minutes.

She adjusted the straps of her red halter top. Red, Carlos's favorite color, looked good on her. She wanted to look good for Carlos.

Sitting down on the beach, digging her toes into the perfectly soft white sand, and watching the light that came from everywhere sparkle on the turquoise sea, she prayed for Carlos to arrive. She really ought to have done something special for this visit. "Baked" brownies, painted her toes and nails, straightened her hair.

Her thirty minutes passed quickly. Still no sign of Carlos. Gina pulled her knees into her chest and counted the clouds. The volleyball game continued. She glanced at the spirits volleying the ball back and forth with carefree bliss and the spectators watching intently. Then one of the spectators rose and approached Gina. A tall and slender older gentleman dressed in a Harvard sweatshirt, shorts and tennis shoes. She recognized him from her last visit to the beach with Carlos. She'd always wondered why he chose to look like he was in his sixties. Most people chose to appear in whatever they considered the prime of their life. She wondered if he'd died at this age, but was too polite to ask.

"Good afternoon, my young one," the gentleman ghost greeted her. "Where is your favorite painter, Carlos?"

Gina gripped a handful of sand into her right fist and tossed it. "I don't know. He is supposed to be here. This is our time and place to meet."

"But you know times and places are ever-changing in Heaven."

Gina felt a wave of anxiety sweep through her.

As if he perceived her distress, the man reassured her, "Don't give up. Maybe I can help you. Carlos is a painter. Look around and try to think like an artist. What would an artist make of this beautiful rocky coast? Do that, and I wouldn't be surprised if you found him." He held out his hand and helped Gina to her feet. Then he tucked her hand into the crook of his elbow and guided her along the edge of the lapping waves.

A little further down the beach, twin teenage girls were building a sand castle. At her companion's suggestion, Gina went over to them and asked, "Have either of you noticed a man around the beach painting or sculpting?"

"Oh, yes," enthused one of the girls. "I remember you and your artist lover from last week. I wish I'd had a soul mate when … you know, when I died."

"So you've seen him?"

"I just noticed him a few hours ago up on the cliffs with an easel, painting the sea." The girl pointed to the rocky outcropping at the end of the beach.

Gina looked up toward the rocky cliffs many yards away. In the distance she could make out a man sitting on the highest rock in front of an easel, holding a paintbrush and making wide sweeping motions across the canvas.

"I see him!" she exclaimed, turning to her gentleman companion.

"So, what are you waiting for?" he wondered.

"I only have fifteen minutes of my visit left. He's too far away. I'll never make it over there in time."

The gentleman smiled. "Time, Gina? What is time, here?"

Gina gazed back toward the cliff. What was time? Something she had neither understood, nor managed well.

Her gentleman companion took her hand. "Fly, Gina. Or, if you cannot yet fly, run as fast as you can."

One of the twins stood and took her other hand. "If you run as fast you can, you can make it. I know you can."

Gina couldn't trust herself to fly, but she could run like the wind. She sprinted toward the cliff, screaming Carlos's name, waving her arms wildly. The sand slipped beneath her feet, impeding her progress. Carlos couldn't seem to hear her. Why couldn't he hear her? He ought to be able to feel her longing, her desperation. She had only squeezed in a few stolen moments with Carlos during her visits over the last several years and today, her time was short.

"Run!" the teenager behind her urged.

"Fly," the gentleman encouraged. His voice filled her mind.

She didn't quite fly, but she felt like she floated over the sand, light as sea foam. She reached the bottom of the outcropping of rocks and looked up. "Carlos!" she shouted.

Now, he turned and looked around for a second as if something had distracted him, then resumed his painting.

He must not see me, Gina thought. She called his name again, then leapt lightly to the rocks.

Now he had heard her, recognized her voice and called out to her, "Gina? Where are you?"

"I'm down here. I'm coming up." She continued to bound upward as if weightless—which, of course, she was.

Carlos appeared at the crown of the cliff, smiling brilliantly down at her. Holding out his hand, his face eager, expectant, and full of love.

But Gina felt the tug at her consciousness that meant her time was up.

"I can't stay," she cried. "I have to go."

Carlos faded as Gina retreated back to Halfway, tears wetting her cheeks.

* * *

Margo withdrew into the shadows along one wall as Eddie entered his son's hospital room. In her mind, she returned to the the night Thomas had taken her to see Eddie and Amy together in his cabin. Looking at Luke now, things fell quickly into place. She remembered the strange sensation she'd had seeing them together that night, the conviction that there were three heartbeats in the room. The baby had been conceived that very night, though she had taken it as a premonition of what was to come.

I felt Luke from the beginning.

Margo looked at Eddie's ring finger. It remained bare, as it had been the last time she had seen him. She had celebrated their divorce once. Now, it saddened her. She hoped that meant she had changed—grown. Her attention turned back to Luke. His lanky body and olive skin resembled Amy. So, too, the arch of his brow, the tilt of his mouth. The soulfulness of his blue eyes, however, was all Eddie.

Eddie sat down in the chair Margo had just vacated and pulled it up next to the bed. "That must have been some fight."

"Yeah, well, that taxi wasn't going down easy," Luke chuckled, and then grabbed his side. "Ouch!"

Margo felt an irresistible pull to be close to both of them. She moved until she stood next to Eddie's chair, then bent down, and stroked Luke's cheek with the palm of her hand.

Luke froze. "She's here," he whispered.

"Who's here?" Eddie asked, looking around the room.

"That girl I told you about."

"And I told you to stop drinking and smoking so much pot. That crap will fry your brain." Eddie squirmed, looking uncomfortable. "If this is the stuff you called me about a few weeks ago, let's drop it."

"Dad, I can't just drop it," Luke uttered. "Hey, believe me, I know it sounds weird. But the thing is, I swear she was there last night when the taxi hit me. She pushed me out of the way. Now, she's here and she's dressed like a doctor, I think. She's a little hard to see."

"Jesus, Luke." Eddie ran his fingers through his hair and laughed nervously. "You're telling me you've seen some kind of ghost flying around your dorm bed and the ghost saved your life?"

"That's exactly what I'm saying. Except she never did any flying." A long moment of silence followed, in which Luke appeared to be staring straight at Margo. She didn't touch him again. She just waited and watched.

A moment of heavy silence ensued. "Dad," Luke began slowly, "tell me about Margo Tracey."

"How do you know about Margo?" Eddie asked, surprised.

"There's a photo on the bookshelf at home of Mom posing arm-in-arm with her high school roommates."

"And?" Eddie stood up wearily from the bedside chair, turned to the window to pull back the blinds, and looked down onto the parking lot several floors below.

"Mom told me the red-haired girl was Margo. She's the girl I've been seeing since I transferred to CHP."

Eddie turned back to stare at Luke, his face pale. For the first time, Margo thought, he looked not just older, but haunted. "The night of the fire," Eddie continued quietly, "I planned to leave an off-campus party with Margo, but, instead, I left with your mother."

"Where did Margo go?"

"Margo went home to Francis Hall with Gina. You know the rest."

"Are you saying that if you'd gone home with Margo and not Mom, that Margo would be alive but Mom wouldn't?"

Eddie shook his head. "No. Your mother always stayed out late, had fun. She would've been fine. But, I believe that if I'd just followed through on something for once, if I'd just left the party with Margo … she'd still be here. Her death was my fault."

No, Eddie. No, Margo thought. *It was mine.*

"Do you ever think about her?" Luke asked.

Margo moved until she was right in front of Eddie, looking into his eyes. She waited for his answer, and finally, it came.

"Yeah, I think about her. A lot. I loved her, Luke. And after that, I loved your mother. Just not enough."

Margo stepped closer to Eddie and traced his lips with the tips of her fingers. The lovely face remained the same. He had loved her, in his own way, in the only way he knew how. His tough, ungraceful disposition was unchanged, still looking like he was a cuss away from a second-rate brawl. But the slight difference in the contours of his features around his eyes and smile comforted her. He frowned, blinked, as if…

"It's not your fault," she whispered in his ear.

"She said it's not your fault," Luke repeated.

"Who said?" Eddie asked, startled.

"Margo," Luke replied, his voice calm.

"Margo's—she's still here?"

"She's right in front of you," Luke explained. "How does that make you feel?"

Eddie raised a hand as if to reach out toward her, but then he put his fingertips to his lips and took a deep breath. "Touched." He sank back into the chair and, burying his face in his hands, he wept.

After a time, he composed himself and took a long deep breath.

"Tell her then, for me, she was always my good luck charm." Eddie pulled something on a chain out of the neck of his shirt. His high school ring still dangled on the long silver chain. Pulling it off over his head, he set it on the table, and left the room.

It seemed sad and lonely to leave, but disorientation was creeping in, putting Margo on the verge of hysteria. She watched Eddie go, then took one last loving look at Luke before she moved into the hall, her entire being drooping with fatigue. She slowly drifted to the floor, oblivious to the activity around her. In the dim hallway, the once crisp patter of nurses and doctors now seemed muted, as if Margo were wearing a set of those big, heavy headphones like they'd had in the language labs at school.

How could Eddie blame himself for her death? It had been her fault. All their deaths had been her fault.

She knelt in the middle of the busy hospital corridor, raised her face to heaven, and cried aloud, "*I did it*! I started the fire! Do you hear me, God? *I* started the fire!"

God knew that—of course, He must have always known it. But she had never been able to confess it. That was her sin, too. She curled into a ball and cried as she had never cried before.

"All these years you've avoided crossing over. Was this why?" The voice, so close it sounded as if it came from her own head, was Thomas, of course.

Margo had no idea how long he had been there. In fact, she had no idea how long she'd been there, huddled against the hospital wall. Minutes, perhaps hours, perhaps days or years. The tears finally stopped. Strange tears—they left no trace, they never fell, they simply evaporated.

She collected herself and slowly rose. Her voice quivered with exhaustion. "Yes, Thomas. Now you know."

He took her trembling hand. "Let's walk."

Red Mittens

She suddenly felt more corporeal, more substantial. She supposed Thomas' presence always did that for her. Thomas gave her … gravity. A sense of belonging in a place she knew she didn't really belong. Not completely, anyway.

They passed the cafeteria and the nurses' lounge and slipped out the door at the end of the hall and into the open air.

"How did it happen?" Thomas asked as he led her along a wide path.

They stopped in front of wooden bench. The sun began to rise and the impatient flowers seemed almost to come awake, to turn their faces to the light. She sat down heavily on the bench, her eyes on the cobblestones of the path.

"It was the red mittens."

Thomas sat down beside her, still holding her hand. "I fail to see how mittens can cause a fire."

"Mittens can cause a fire when a careless student leaves them in front of a propped-up hairdryer in a dorm bathroom. They were wet. I left the bathroom to put on my pajamas and forgot about them. When they dried out, they must have caught fire. Or maybe the electric cord was faulty. Either way, I must have left the dryer on." She felt all sense of her "life," as she'd come to comprehend it, draining from her body.

"So that's your understanding of the cause?" Thomas asked. "You never heard the speculation that a nightlight sparked in a bad socket, or a bit of bad wiring in a closet light fixture combusted? I heard both of those theories in my travels … and from some of your companions in death."

"Theorizing isn't going to make this better, Thomas. I *know* I'm the culprit. My mother knitted me that pair of red mittens at the beginning of my sophomore year. I wore them all the time."

Thomas regarded her solemnly. "So many times, for so many years, I pleaded with you to tell me what you've been holding inside. And you hid this secret all these years? From me—even from God?"

Margo looked up at Thomas. "You can't hide things from God. I get that. I was hiding it from myself … along with other things."

"Which was why it took a reunion with your beloved Eddie to bring this to the forefront. Or was it the near death of his son?"

She nodded. "When I think of him, I'm still alive. When I think of him, I'm in love and, if only for a brief moment, I forget about the red mittens. And when I sent medical discoveries to Earth, I felt I might have a chance to redeem myself."

That was never going to happen, but at least her secret was out in the open now—the whole gory history she had hidden in her soul for nineteen years. She felt … relief. It bloomed inside her, big and fine—as if she were filling with air, becoming lighter. Thomas knew the truth; soon Gina would know it as well.

I'm going to Hell.

Thomas slipped from his seat and knelt in front of Margo, bringing her hands to his lips for a kiss. "Why didn't you just tell me?" he asked. "I could have helped you."

"For a while, I thought you knew. I thought you must know. If God knew…"

Thomas shook his head. "God does. Guides in Halfway don't. Your souls have to tell us what's holding you back—once you discover what that is. Or, if you know, you have to grow in courage enough to speak of it."

"I felt helpless, Thomas," she told him. "I was terrified of crossing over, because I knew I couldn't be headed to the same destination as Gina … and eventually, Eddie."

"You don't know that. You're playing judge and jury without all the facts." Thomas tilted his head to one side. "What about now? Do you still fear that?"

"Now, I'm resigned to it. And now, I realize how horribly selfish I've been. My God, I only compounded my sins by holding Gina back all this time."

Thomas nodded. "Gina may have held herself back for a time, even if you didn't. And I suspect she learned much about herself in the process. But now, you do know what you have to do, despite the outcome, yes?"

Margo gripped his hands more tightly. "Can't Gina cross over without me? I want to stay here with you. Maybe I could be a guide, too. It's not like I don't know my way around after all these years."

He put a finger to her lips. "You know the rules. You are bound to each other."

Margo tried to pull her hands away, but Thomas held them tightly and made her meet his gaze. "There are other considerations, you know."

"Like what?" Margo asked.

"What about your medical findings? Just think of all those volumes of scientific and medical knowledge you could funnel directly to living scientists from the Light. Your work will bear no fruit if it's not planted in the world of humanity. Humanity needs that knowledge."

Margo sighed. "My work doesn't seem important anymore."

"Margo," Thomas promised in a low voice, "you can change the world, but not from here. Not from Halfway. Souls in Halfway are prevented from having far-reaching effects. Only from Heaven can you shed light on the physical world." He dropped her hands and, leaning forward, kissed her gently. "It's time for you to move on."

She finally heard what he said and understood its full import. "Heaven—no, I … You can't believe I'd go to the Light. I'm going to the Fire."

"You don't know that. It's not my decision. If it were, you'd have been in the Light long ago. But this is God's decision: You will go where you belong."

"What about you? Isn't that why you've been in Halfway for centuries? Fear of Hell?" She drew her head back and looked at him levelly. "Isn't it?"

Thomas lowered his gaze. "That's between me and God. And my record is, shall we say, a bit darker than yours. You may have accidentally brought death to people you loved. I intentionally brought it to people I … cared little about. And I brought death to the people I loved through negligence and greed. I am, most certainly, bound for Hell."

"You don't know that, and besides, isn't that God's decision to make?" she asked, echoing his words to her. "Doesn't the service you've done souls through your guidance count against your sins? You've certainly learned love. Isn't that the most important thing?"

"I doubt I've learned enough to save my soul."

"Look at me," Margo demanded. When he did, she gazed deeply into his blue eyes. "Go where you belong. Go to your wife, Lydia, and your daughter, Pearl. Whatever's been stopping you, don't let it stop you any longer."

"I told you, my sins stop me, Margo!" the cry seemed wrenched from the depths of his soul. "I murdered fellow pirates and honest merchants in cold blood—or in the fires of greed. I slit their throats while they cried for mercy. I bathed in their blood. The only place for me is at the bottommost levels of Hell."

"But you've owned your sins and done your penance. You've spent hundreds of years in Halfway, leading other souls to their ultimate goal. Leading me to mine. You've been so patient, so kind."

He paused silently for a moment, then wondered aloud, "It's a curious thought. If it means that much to you, I will think about it."

"Then you will come. To the Cross-over ceremony."

He smiled, drawing her to her feet, then leaned back and gave her once over, laughing, "Well, would you look at that! You're luminous."

"Look at what?" She glanced down at herself and noticed immediately what he was talking about: she no longer wore the nightgown that had been her garment through much of her time here. Now she glowed in a radiant white floor length dress with beading about the neckline. A cream-colored ribbon held her hair in a loose bun.

"I believe," Thomas chided gently, "that even you know you're ready."

Looking into Thomas's beloved face, Margo didn't know whether to laugh or cry.

16

THE DORM ROOM IN Halfway looked the same as always. Gazing about as she woke, Margo wondered why it always appeared like that. What if, for example, she wanted the walls to be—oh, lime green, say?

The walls were lime green.

She shook her head. Why had it taken her so long to assimilate what Thomas had been trying to tell her from day one—that her thoughts were her reality here. She'd worn that damned nightgown for so long because…

She stopped to think about that, realizing at last the complexity behind that choice. Perhaps recognizing—or at least really *getting*—that it *was* a choice. The nightgown served as a familiar souvenir of her physical life. She had died in it—being the last garment she'd worn made it special. Loved … and loathed. It served as a symbol of her guilt and a memorial to her human existence.

And now—

She perused the sunny room with its lime green walls and understood that what she held in her soul was remembrance enough.

"Margo ... what did you do?" Gina stood in the doorway leading to the bathroom, gawping at the walls.

Margo laughed. "I was in the mood for a change."

Gina, who had taken to the idea that clothing could be changed at will long ago, flipped the red cardigan that elegantly matched her dress over one shoulder and narrowed her eyes. "You're in a rare mood. What sort of change did you have in mind?"

"I thought this would be a good day to go check out the commencement ceremony."

"Any particular reason?" Gina inquired.

Margo shrugged, moving to her chest of drawers and pulling out her favorite sweater, the forest green one that set off her hair. Soon that sort of thing wouldn't matter. There wouldn't be sweaters or hairstyles needed to complement where either of them were going.

"Well, considering that we have an application in, I figure we should really be there to confirm our intentions."

Gina's face lit up. "An application? You put in an application for visitor's passes?"

Margo pulled the sweater on and smoothed it over her hips. "No. I put in an application to cross over."

"What?" Gina's cardigan slipped from her shoulder to the floor.

Margo lifted it with a flick of her hand and flew it across the room into her own hands. Gina followed it, not even commenting that Margo didn't usually do things like that.

"You're kidding, right? Don't play games with me, Margo. You know how badly I want to be with Carlos."

Margo sobered. Gina had every reason not to trust her. "We'd better hurry. Wouldn't want to be late to our own commencement."

Red Mittens

Gina stopped right in front of her and took the red sweater out of her hands. "You're serious. You've really done it? Oh, Margo!"

Margo found herself crushed in a tremendous hug and spun in a loopy circle.

"Seriously," she laughed, "let's get going." She turned to pull a pair of blue jeans out of her chest of drawers, then slid into them. She had always worn these with the forest green sweater and a pair of Wallabies that she loved. She savored the sensation of fabric on skin.

She went to her desk next and took out her research—the knowledge Thomas assured her would revolutionize medicine. She put that into the yellow suitcase she had arrived here with, and knew by instinct that her contribution had only just begun, whether in Heaven or in Hell.

Gina sat down on her bed and slipped her feet into a pair of candy-apple red pumps. She stopped futzing with her belt buckle and watched Margo put all of her papers into her suitcase. "Are you scared?"

Margo stared out the window for a moment. "Maybe just a little. But Thomas will be with us. He's going to attempt to cross over with us as well."

"What do you mean *attempt*?" Gina asked.

"We should get going."

At last, they stood on the lawn outside their dorm in a pure wash of non-sunlight, looking back at the big, brick building.

My heavenly dorm, Margo thought. They were the last ones to leave it. All of the other girls that had arrived with them had been gone for ages. They walked off arm-in-arm, Margo carrying her little yellow suitcase full of knowledge—clothes for eternity.

"You know," Gina reminded her, "Eddie's going to be taking his own path to the Light one of these days."

Margo nodded. "I know. I hope … I hope I'm ready for that."

They were crossing the sward at the Crossroads when Margo remarked quietly, "Gina, I'm sorry I gave Carlos the wrong date for the Blind Date Ball."

"Yeah, I know. But that wasn't your fault. You were just …"

"Wrapped up in my own needs," Margo confirmed. "I was careless, with a lot of things. Careless with myself, too. I guess that was my token rebellion." She closed her eyes for a moment and shook off the heaviness of loss.

They settled themselves in the first row on the Crossroads green, facing one end of the oval track. As always, the seats were white folding chairs like the ones found at a high school graduation.

Tradition, Margo thought. *I guess you don't mess with it.*

Margo had never seen the commencement field from this vantage point before. The thought caused her one more wriggle of angst. The structure at the head of the oval wasn't quite what Margo had expected the one time she'd snuck in and watched a ceremony from beneath the bleachers. The part that resembled the shell of the Hollywood Bowl and the flight of stairs descending from it looked like … well, they looked like nothing Margo had ever seen. They seemed to be white marble one moment, crystal the next, then made of rainbows, then of burnished gold, then of precious gems, then of pure light.

The shell itself seemed full of radiant clouds that flowed, eddied and spiraled, like water. The movement reminded Margo of the alien clouds from *Close Encounters of the Third Kind*—the last movie she'd seen.

It also reminded her of fire, and she had to fight the urge to cringe away. She made herself think of it as a Stephen Spielberg sky—it was that alien. And yet, hadn't she always known what it would be like?

"Wow," Gina exhaled next to her. "Who knew? It just looks like a really pretty concert shell from the bleachers."

"Yeah, I know," Margo agreed, scanning the area for Thomas.

Gina shot her a sidewise glance, but didn't utter a word.

As the bleachers filled with people, Margo glanced over her shoulder and observed several ranks of spirits behind them in groups, ones and twos. Some prayed, some absorbed their surroundings, peering at the bleachers, while others stared straight ahead.

The roil of glory in the concert shell become purest white, which meant, Margo knew, that every color of the spectrum was present in it. The radiance somehow parted to reveal the members of the Soul Cleansing Board and several others.

Gina made a sound like a sob and grabbed Margo's arm. "Carlos!"

Margo blinked. Yes, one of the people on the steps was Carlos. Funny, because he seemed to *become* Carlos, as if his form collected around him from the contents of the tilted bowl behind him. He stood just as Margo remembered him—young, dark, handsome, serious-looking. Wearing jeans and a cable-knit sweater—probably the last thing Gina had seen him in.

Margo glanced aside at her friend. Tears filled her eyes and a huge, brilliant smile lit up her face. When Margo looked back at the top of the stairs, she spied her own father. An instant later, she realized that as the Cleansing Board and their "guests" descended the staircase, Thomas had appeared on the bottommost tier to greet them.

The next thing Margo knew, she stood motionless at the

base of the steps, herself, clutching Gina's hand as if she might never let go.

Wow, they sure know how to cut to the chase, don't they?

Victor, the head of the Soul Cleansing Board, spoke directly to Margo: "Thomas has fully informed us of your desire and readiness to cross over. He feels you have at last faced those fears and let go of those attachments that have kept you here. I admit, seeing your choice of garments does much to underscore his testimony."

He smiled. The not-sunlight seemed to brighten.

"Now," he continued, "I must ask you, Margo Tracey: have you left behind your fear that your ultimate destiny may not be full Light?"

She nodded. "I have."

"Why do you wish to undertake this transition?"

Margo glanced at Gina, who just managed to take her eyes from Carlos long enough to meet her gaze. "Because I held Gina back. Keeping her from love, light, and healing. I trapped her with me in my own guilt and despair. I want to set her free. And I want to be free, myself, even if it means ... I go someplace else."

"Wait a minute!" Gina raised her hand between Margo and Victor, waving it up and down as if to cut off the conversation. "Why in Heaven's name—pardon the expression—should Margo not go to the Light too? Why would she go to Darkness? I mean, if anyone deserves to go to Hell, it's me with my-my stupid, acting out and-and my infantile tantrums and my obsession with sex. Margo's a *saint* compared to me!"

Victor started to reply but Gina cut him off—something Margo might have found amusing if Victor had been a librarian or a professor or even a police officer and not the head of the Soul Cleansing Board that would decide the merit of her friend's readiness for the spiritual realms.

"I'm not done yet. Look, Margo died in that fire because she went back to save people. She could've escaped, but she didn't. She went back and got them out and-and then it was too late. Then, we couldn't come down the stairs."

To Margo's horror, the scars of the fire were creeping back to mar Gina's perfect skin. The horrible scent of charred hair and flesh swirled around her.

"Margo died trying to save people," Gina finished through twisted lips.

"Gina," Margo whispered softly. "Gina, I started that fire in the first place."

"What?" Gina stared at her blankly.

"I didn't know it at the time. But later, when we went back, the news stories suggested the fire ignited in our bathroom … that there was a hairdryer left plugged in and turned on." Margo felt so cold, suddenly. So cold and empty. The expression on Gina's face had gutted her. "My mittens did it, Gina. The red mittens my mother knitted. I must have put them in front of a hairdryer to dry, then forgot about them and went to bed."

Gina frowned, shaking her head. "I remember you asked me to get them for you when I went back up for my hat and gloves, but I—" She stopped, her gaze locking with Margo's and not letting go. "Is that what this has been about, really, all these years? A pair of red mittens?"

Margo nodded.

Gina's face suddenly appeared scar free. Margo smelled her perfume—jasmine and orange blossom. "Margo, you idiot. Why didn't you tell me before—nineteen years ago, maybe?"

"What difference—"

"I never found your mittens, damnit—pardon my French," she added with a glance at Victor. "I came back empty-handed and you walked to the dance with your hands in your pockets."

"But on the way back—"

"I let you wear my gloves on the way back, remember? I felt bad, 'cause I didn't find your mittens. Come to think of it, I don't remember seeing those mittens all year."

Margo shook her head. "No, that ... that can't be. The stories mentioned a hairdryer left on. It overheated—"

"It wasn't your mittens. It wasn't her mittens, sir," she repeated, turning to Victor. "She didn't kill anybody. Not even by accident."

"It's true, sweetie."

Margo looked up and saw that her father had come down the gleaming steps to stand on the tread just above Victor and a bit to one side. He had something in his hands.

"We found these in your room at home."

She stared at what he held out to her: the mittens, soft, bright, red. Not really the mittens, she knew, but the way she had last seen them.

"I think you meant to pack them," Gyp explained, "and they fell off the bed. They were ... they were just under the edge of the bedspread. We didn't realize that because we'd closed up your room for so long. It took almost five years before we'd healed enough to go in and pack your things away."

I didn't cause the fire.

For Margo, the entire universe seemed to stop in its movement. She let herself be suspended there for a long moment, then looked up at Victor.

He smiled kindly. "Do you believe him, Margo?" he asked.

"Of course, I believe him."

"Then what holds you here?"

Margo looked at Gina, at her father, who stood one step closer to the Light with his hand extended toward her.

"It's time, honey," he beckoned. "Time for you to come home with me."

Victor, still smiling, opened his hand. Balanced in it—or over it—was a brilliant spark of pure light. He set the spark over Margo's heart and there it stayed, suffusing her with light and warmth and acceptance.

From the corner of her eye, Margo saw the Board member facing Gina give her the same gift—her permanent passkey to the next realm.

She moved then, taking a step upward, feeling Gina's hand tighten in hers. As she rose toward her father, she saw someone else standing within the wash of glory at the top of the steps—a woman and a girl and a young man. She recognized Thomas's wife, Lydia, and his daughter, Pearl, and the light of longing in their eyes. The young man must be the son he had tried to find on his last voyage.

She turned to Thomas, who followed several steps below her now. "Thomas, look, it's your family! They're waiting for you. They've come here to take you home too."

Thomas looked up at the little group with tears in his eyes. A smile trembled on his lips, but he shook his head. "One day, I'll pass that way, but for now, I need a bit more time. Keep an eye out for me, though. You never know when you might run into an overbearing pirate."

Margo hesitated, wavering on her step. The Light washed over her, bearing her up toward the bowl of glory.

Thomas made a shooing gesture at her. "Go. Your father's right. It's time. And as much as it pains me to say it, Victor's right too. There should be nothing to hold you here now. You've done enough penance for both of us, when none was needed."

Margo smiled, already feeling the threads of attachment falling away. She could feel the Light pulsing through her, vaguely aware of music coming from nowhere and everywhere at once.

Then *He* appeared to take Margo and Gina in His arms and draw them fully into the Light. Where they belonged.

Made in the USA
Middletown, DE
28 October 2018